The Prisoner

Matthew Holt

Contents

1 Waking Up

2 Going Home

3 Down Memory Lane

4 Plans Are Made

5 Finding an Old Friend

6 Transformed!

7 Duties

8 Midridge

9 Preparations and Excavations

10 Questions

11 Invasion!

12 Evasion

13 A Powerful Ally

14 A Secret Revealed

15 A Final Reckoning

16 Picking Up The Pieces

17 A Familiar Face

18 Damsel In Distress, Again!

Chapter 1

Waking Up

Hillbrook Corporation's Forest View Medical Center

Cloudsmoor District

Southern Continent

Planet Cestus, Altair System

Susan

I woke up slowly, feeling very weak and disoriented. I felt like my head was full of wool. It was hard to think clearly. As my mind slowly woke up and cleared I found myself in a hospital bed in what was obviously an ICU private room, albeit a very luxurious one. My bed was surrounded by top-of-the-line support equipment. Various feeds and leads were connected to me, snaking from the machines around me to vanish under the thin blanket. An oxygen mask was covering my nose and mouth.

Whatever pain relief I was being given must have been top notch because I did not feel any pain or discomfort. I could still feel and move my limbs, albeit feebly so they hadn't fitted me with a neural block. I thought that was a good sign. It likely meant I hadn't lost any limbs or been severely burned. I could feel substantial dressings around my body and support frames around my legs, so my injuries had still been bad. I did not have the strength to lift the thin blanket and see exactly how bad.

My memory of the accident was still hazy. I could recall the explosion and fire in the shuttle and the smell of smoke and burning plastic and metal. I could vaguely recall that my father had ordered me into the last escape pod, but I had refused. I had not wanted to leave my parents. The other escape pods had been destroyed by the explosion that had wrecked the shuttle's engines and put it on an uncontrollable descent through the atmosphere of Cestus.

Had the shuttle survived? The fact that I was alive meant maybe we had all made it. I prayed with all my heart that we had.

Eventually my return to consciousness must have been noticed as a nurse came into my field of view to check on me. It was an android, of course. A high functioning series eleven model or higher from what I could see. Its polished metallic body was humanoid and its synthetic face was carefully sculpted to inspire trust and confidence in its patients. Over its chrome and steel body it wore a spotless nurse's scrubs.

"Please don't try to move, Mistress Susan." It said. Its voice soft, gentle and caring. "You suffered severe injuries, and the regeneration process will have left you feeling very weak. Just try to rest."

Regeneration?, how badly had I been hurt that I needed regeneration? Maybe I had been wrong about my assessment of how badly I had been injured. Regeneration was used only in the most severe of cases. When new organs or whole limbs needed to be re-grown. I couldn't remember any more from the accident aside from a few mental images of the shuttle shaking, flames and my parent's yelling and pleading with me to get into the last escape pod. Had I finally done so? Had I escaped and left my parents to die?

"What happened?" I asked, my voice was so weak it was barely more than a croaking whisper, "Did my parents survive?"

"Please don't try to talk." Said the nurse. "When you are feeling better someone will be here to talk to you."

In other words, it wasn't going to give me bad news when I was still very ill. My heart sank and a creeping despair took hold of me. If they had survived there would have been no reason not to tell me. I felt tears coming and the nurse must have noticed and altered my level of sedation as I remembered nothing more.

When I next woke up, I was starting to feel a little better. The feeling of weakness was much reduced and there seemed to be fewer leads connected to me. I expect they had kept me sedated for quite some time as the support frames were gone from my legs and the dressings were much reduced in size. The nurse must have lowered my sedation as she was standing ready, obviously awaiting my return to consciousness.

"How do you feel?" it asked in that same soft gentle voice.

"hmm ..better." I replied. My own voice sounded a little stronger.

The nurse busied itself with alterations to my medication and dressings. It was calm, caring and, of course, competent to the point of perfection. All androids were, of course. I wanted to ask about my parents but was afraid to hear the answer I knew would be coming.

"If you feel up to it, Mistress Susan, there is someone who wishes to speak with you."

"Who is it?" I asked.

"I am informed he is an agent of the legal firm employed by your parents. He is waiting to talk to you by holo, if you are willing." The nurse's told

My stomach felt like it was filled with lead. There was only one reason why a lawyer would want to talk to me in this situation. I guess I was about to get answer to my question. I knew what was coming, but was I strong enough to have it confirmed?

I gathered myself together. "OK." I said, "I'll talk to him."

The nurse withdrew, perhaps to provide the illusion of privacy. Though I knew a whole slew of monitoring systems would be active in this room all the time. Beside my bed there appeared the usual purple glow hanging in the air that always preceded a holo projection and then the full figure of the lawyer appeared.

It was, like the nurse, an android. It had a duller metallic finish to its body, a combination of bronze and brushed steel, and actually wore a business suit! Its face was sculpted in the classic serious male pattern so common to androids that had to deal formally with humans.

"Greeting Mistress Susan. My name is Thadeus GN70131." It said, "I am an authorised legal agent of Grissom and Taylor, the legal firm retained by your mother and father. I am here in accordance with specific instructions from your parents."

His voice was calm and melodious. The perfect tone selected for a lawyer giving their client bad news.

"Is my father ..." I paused, .."my parents?.."

"I am sorry to be the bearer of such news, but I have to tell you that your parents did not survive the destruction of your shuttle. I understand from your company's investigators that they did manage to get you into a life-pod. Unfortunately, the pod was also damaged by the fire on the shuttle, so your own descent ended in a crash landing. Your injuries were very serious."

I closed my eyes and clenched my fists. I had known this news was coming but it still hurt more than I could stand. Thadeus waited patiently.

Eventually I was able to talk. "How long.. how long have I been here?"

"The incident took place twenty six days ago." He replied, "You have been here ever since a Hillbrook security team found and retrieved you from the remains of the life-pod."

Thadeus paused to let me absorb that information before continuing. "There is important information I must share with you, in accordance with my instructions. If you feel strong enough?"

I nodded.

"Your father's and mother's last wills and testament named you as their sole heir. This has been ratified by the probate court here on Cestus and by the Commonwealth Corporate Holdings Register back on Earth. You are now the owner of their entire estates and of course that includes their majority stake in Hillbrook Cybernetics."

This came as no surprise to me. My father had raised me to one day take his place as head of the corporation that he and my mother owned. Though I am sure he did not anticipate it happening this way, or this soon.

Thadeus continued, "As you are currently only twenty-three years of age you are, under Commonwealth law, still too young to be in charge of your own affairs. You will not be able to control your own estate or make legal decisions on your own behalf until your twenty fifth birthday."

This too I understood. Over that last few centuries, advances in medical science had extended the average human lifespan well beyond one hundred years. The age at which someone was officially considered an adult had likewise been increased in proportion.

"This brings me to the question of the appointment of a guardian. Your mother and father were adamant that none of the remaining members of your family would be suitable. They are too distantly related to know you well enough, or, in the opinion of your parents, to be trusted with your care. He also made it clear that the security situation made it imperative that any selected guardian must be absolutely trustworthy. To the point of being incorruptible" Explained Thadeus.

The security situation my father referred to was the dangerous world in which we lived. Commonwealth law in theory held sway across human controlled space. But the reality was that the huge corporations held the real power in all the inhabited systems beyond Earth itself. They vied for power, trade, technology and whatever advantage they could achieve using every means at their disposal, whether legal or otherwise.

Alongside sabotage, industrial espionage and bribery, assassination was a key corporate tool. The destruction of our shuttle, I guessed, had been such an assassination attempt. I would now be the prime target. I had no remaining close relatives so if I was killed the ownership of our company, one of the largest cybernetics corporations in the Commonwealth, would be the subject of a chaotic war of competing claims by my distant cousins. It would cripple the company and our rivals would take advantage.

Anyone appointed as my guardian would need to be incorruptible. I wondered what my parents had decided. Thadeus, had the answer.

"Albeit an unusual measure, your parents stipulated that only a cybernetic entity specifically designed for the task could fulfil the role of guardian. Therefore, a series sixteen android is being constructed who will act as your legal guardian until you reach your twenty-fifth birthday." it explained.

"An android! An android is going to be my guardian?" I asked, stunned.

"That is correct. The android in question will be the highest specification android ever produced by your company's orbital fabrication facilities." Said Thadeus.

"But is it even legal? Androids cannot own property." I protested.

"That is correct, but there is no legal objection to an android acting as a legal guardian. Despite having the legal guardianship authority accorded by the court, it will not actually be owning any property. The entire estate will remain yours, but the guardian will have legal authority over it until your twenty fifth birthday" Explained Thadeus.

"But this means this android will have control over our company!" I objected.

Thadeus nodded, "Officially, yes. But I am sure your own input will be respected. Plus, the company board will still have direct control of the day-to-day business. Your guardian will not be able to do anything against your own best interest. It will be constrained by the behavioural controls in its programming. Your father and mother considered this the best solution and the courts have ratified this decision."

I sighed, "Meaning there is nothing I can do?"

Thadeus shook its head solemnly, "There is nothing you can do to change the court's decision. I would suggest you defer judgement on your new guardian until you have met it.

"And when will that be?"

"The medical team here have, in accordance with restrictions on confidentiality, been keeping us informed of your progress. Their current medical assessment is that you will be well enough to leave the hospital in nine days. By that time your guardian will have been completed and will be waiting for you at your family estate." Explained Thadeus.

Wanting to change the subject I asked, "Did they find out who sabotaged our shuttle?"

Thadeus shook his head, "You would have to ask your own company's investigators. They have no obligation to communicate their findings to myself or any other representative of our firm."

"But it was obviously sabotage?" I asked.

Thadeus held up on hand defensively, "I cannot make that determination. Though an explosion on a shuttle that did not carry anything explosive is very suspicious."

In other words, it considered it obvious that it was sabotage. I felt the same way. Our shuttle had had a very high capacity grav engine. There was no combustible fuel of any kind on board. Certainly nothing that could explode. Grav engines were solid state technology. They used a zero-point quantum power source. If that failed in any way the engine would just stop working, it would not explode. No, this had been a deliberate attempt to kill us.

With nothing more TO say the lawyer made his excuses, wished me a speedy recovery, and cut the connection.

I lay with a sick empty feeling in my stomach. My parents were gone. They had been my whole world. In this world where threats were everywhere, and no human could be trusted, I had been brought up in isolation. The threat of assassination or kidnap had ruled out me going to any kind of school with other kids. I had been educated by AR systems and android tutors. Aside from my parents themselves, my playmates from my earliest days had either been virtual creations in AR or cybernetic.

The only time I had spent time with other children were the very rare social interactions with the leaders of other companies, or senior politicians and their families. Those events had been so formalised and restricted by security they could never be described as fun. All my happiest memories were when I had spent time just with my parents. Just the three of us.

How could I face life now without them? I had terrible sense of loneliness. When I was released from the care of this hospital I would be returning to our family home. A home that would now only be occupied my me. Our home estate was immense. It would feel horrible and strange to be the only human in it. The only life.

The idea of having an android guardian should not have bothered me. I had grown up surrounded by androids. They were the world I knew. What I was comfortable with. Their loyalty guaranteed by their programming.

Androids were known and reliable. No human servants, companions or guards of any kind were allowed near the family. Humans could be bribed. When rival companies could put almost unlimited funds into corrupting someone there were few who could resist. For those few who could not be bought there was also the option of threats, either to them or their families.

The androids I had known all my life had all been the creations of my family's own company. We were the premier manufacturer of cybernetic products in the Commonwealth.

The rapid expansion of the Commonwealth had outstripped the capacity of the human race to increase their numbers to match. Corporations, keen to maximise their profits were opening up new worlds all the time and that process created a huge demand for labour that humanity could not fulfil. Thus, the market for our company's products was immense. Our company made its money by manufacturing all kinds of cybernetic entities. From domestic androids to thousand-ton space-faring mining mechs.

I should start thinking of it as my company now. My father and mother together had owned eighty percent of the stock. It was mine now. Just like all the other assets of my family. Even though I could not actively control any of it for nearly another two years.

What was life with an android guardian going to be like? Would it try to boss me around? In theory its behavioural controls should require it to obey any lawful order given it by its owner, which I assumed was me. Did that mean it could not order me to do anything? I had studied android law and behavioural controls during my education but after racking my brains I could not remember anything covering the question of an android giving orders to a human. Any human. Let alone their owner. Just what actual authority could an android guardian have?

I resolved to look up the relevant law before I arrived at the estate and met my new guardian face to face.

Chapter 2

Going Home

Getting from the medical centre to my family estate was not a simple operation. Once the centre had deemed itself satisfied that I was healthy enough to leave their care a complex security operation swung into action.

I was used to this. I had grown up surrounded by security. The difference now was that before I had always been with my parents. Now I was alone, and all the security effort was entirely centred around me.

If I had been an ordinary citizen of Cestus, or of any other Commonwealth world, I would have been able to book a flight either on an internal commercial flight or book a private flight on a flyer controlled by an AI. For someone who owned a vast business empire and was almost certainly going to be the target of seriously well organised and capable assassination attempts getting from one place to another was nothing short of a major military operation.

The security division of the company was staffed entirely by androids and security drones of our own manufacture, along with other assets all under AI control. A fleet of well-armed combat drones would escort my flight back to the estate. They would all focus on defending the main transport which was a large, heavily armoured, and armed flyer.

The Forest View Medical facility was located underground at one of our companies main dirtside manufacturing facilities. I left the hospital complex in an AI controlled grav-car which took me to a vast underground hangar. This was where our fleet was assembled. I alighted from the car and was met by a high specification android. This, I assumed, was the android in charge of my security.

"Welcome Mistress Susan, I am Julius DX10273." It said in greeting.

That name rang a bell for me, "Hello Julius, I remember you from last time we were home on Cestus. Are we ready to go?"

Julies nodded, "I am gratified you remember me, Mistress Susan. Yes, we have received clearance from our surveillance assets that there are no nearby surface or airborne threats detected. If you will just board your flyer we should leave before that changes."

Julies was surely keen to see us on the move before any threats emerged. I heeded its words and strode quickly over to my flyer and climbed aboard. Several sets of massive doors opened above us, and our armada took off and rapidly climbed to reach as high a cruising altitude as it could reach.

The security division had satellite, ground and airborne drone scanners to cover our entire route, but it was best to fly high so that if any attack was launched, we would have as much warning as possible.

I sat back in my seat and tried not to think of the vast and expensive operation going on around me. The whole thing just designed to get me safely from one location to another on a single planet. Something ordinary folk could do with no worries at all.

There were no external windows on the flyer, but conveniently placed screens showed a range of images. I could select any view from any of the craft in our fleet or even from other company assets nearby. I decided to do what I usually did on a long flight, select some relaxing music and try to get some sleep. Thinking too hard about the details of what was going on around me would just keep me awake.

However, I had been dozing for no more than a few minutes when a sudden powerful acceleration woke me up. The seat harness automatically tightened, and I gripped the armrests fiercely as the flyer threw itself into some wild manoeuvres.

A coms link came active and Julius's relaxed and professional voice said, "Please remain calm, Mistress Susan. At attack has been detected and we are manoeuvring to evade. I apologise for any discomfort."

I looked at the camera feeds and I saw our whole fleet was moving to avoid a series of incoming missile tracks. The escort drones fired interception missiles of their own. The main transport also loosed missiles and all of our fleet accelerated and dove to confuse the incoming guided weapons, weaving and jinking to make themselves difficult targets.

'Discomfort' was something I was quite happy to endure if it meant I arrived home safely. As my craft manoeuvred the g-forces grew. Even though I was accustomed to space-travel and had been given extensive training in managing g-stress I was being pushed to my limit. The seat extended padded baffles to hold my head still and extra padded straps snapped around my arms and legs. Through the strain of all the twists and turns I kept my eye on the screens that showed the incoming missiles.

As they got closer our own counter-missiles found their mark, blowing the enemy projectiles apart in bright flashes of fire and debris. As the scanners updated, I could see that a few hostile weapons had made it through. Shorter range particle beams lanced out from all our ships to try and stop the incoming threat. All but one missile was destroyed but that single one struck home. Blowing the nose off the main transport flyer. It began to tumble out of control, pieces falling free as it was consumed by fire and further explosions. Becoming a shower of burning debris as its remains fell to the ground far below.

Tucked safely inside one of the escorting drones, I watched the decoy ship's destruction. It was a rather old trick, but effective in this case. It was worth forgoing the comparative luxury of the transport for the more anonymous safety of a small compartment hidden inside one of the many combat drones. If my unidentified attackers suspected that they had failed and wished to launch a second strike, they would not know which craft to target.

The security forces of my company would be tracking the source of the missiles and hopefully making sure there would be no more headed our way.

My fleet of drones continued the rest of the way to the estate at low altitude. The extra restraints retracted, and I could at least sit more comfortably once more. I saw an update on my screens telling me that extra drones were coming to provide cover as we travelled the rest of the way home.

Julius's voice came over coms once again "The attack has ended, Mistress Susan. I must sadly confirm that we have lost the main transport decoy. Additional combat forces are being added to our force to provide extra protection. We have traced the source of the attack to a group of mobile launchers hidden in woodland. We have dispatched forces to deal with them."

I watched reports come in from the dispatched security force that it had found that the launchers had self-destructed shortly after firing their missiles. Security division analysts would examine the remains, but I am sure they would find nothing.

The corporate rivals who had planned and resourced this attack were far too clever, and far too experienced to ever leave any trace that could identify them.

This was my reality now, the same reality my family had lived with all our lives. If our rivals could kill me then the ownership of our company would be fought over in court by my various surviving distant relatives. Perhaps the company would even have to be broken up. This would be to the huge advantage of Hillbrook Cybernetics's many rivals, one or more of whom were certainly complicit in the assassinations.

It wasn't personal. There was no malice involved, no hatred. It was just the way business was done in the outer reaches of the Commonweath. The endless round of competition among the most powerful corporations in a universe where wealth and power meant more than the rule of law.

The remainder of the flight passed without further incident. The AI pilot informed me when we were approaching the estate. I activated a screen to show me my home as we approached. From a distance my family estate was deceptive. It looked like a large area of landscaped woodland and meadows, but with a large but very old-fasioned, traditional looking mansion in the centre. In reality this was probably the most heavily defended location on the planet. As our fleet approach the edge of the estate all the drones split off from our formation leaving only the one containing me.

The AI controlling it communicated the correct security codes and a glowing outline of a circular portal appeared ahead of us. This was an opening in the incredibly powerful force field that protected the estate. Or rather force fields as my drone had to navigate through three more such fields before it could approach the main house.

These fields were projected from deep underneath the estate and powered by a fusion reactor system that could provide enough power to run a small city. In theory nothing could get through the force fields, not even an asteroid impact.

A large pair of doors opened in the courtyard at the rear of the house and the drone descended through the exposed opening into an immense subterranean hanger. Once safely on the ground, more security codes were exchanged and the door to the drone opened to allow me to exit.

I unstrapped myself from the seat and climbed carefully out of the cramped compartment just as the doors far overhead closed once more with a resounding boom.

"Home at last." I said out loud.

The shuttle flight that had ended in disaster had been the last leg on a long journey as my parents had visited our company's orbital manufacturing facilities in numerous different systems. A trip that had taken more than a year. It had been a long time since I had set foot in our family home.

Of course, the many androids and other cybernetic entities that ran the estate had kept everything in perfect order. Nothing would have changed since I was last here.

Well one huge thing had changed. The hole left by my parents was still raw and painful. I knew that being home would bring memories flooding back everywhere I went, reminding me of them. This was all part of the grieving process, I knew. But knowing this made it no less painful.

And, of course, one other thing had changed. I wondered how my new guardian would choose to greet me. I did not even know what it looked like.

As I strode across the expanse of the landing bay I saw an android walking toward me. It was certainly one I did not recognise. Was this my new guardian?

It was tall and the metallic sheen of its skin was a combination of shades of bronze. The hallmark of a very high-end model android. It was wearing a simple business suit and its face was, like all such high-level androids, pleasant, calm and reassuring.

It had long been forbidden by law for any android to be made that even approximated human appearance. The technology existed that could build an android that would appear indistinguishable from a natural human. The possibility for abuse of such technology had created such a strong backlash from the general Commonwealth populace that the law on android appearance had been established.

For most androids this meant they had shiny metallic bodies. Chrome being by far the most common finish. Finishes of more subtle colouring had come to be associated with the more expensive and capable models. The law also stipulated that all androids had to be referred to by inanimate pronouns. An android was an 'it', not a 'he' or a 'she'. I thought this law was foolish and part of the prejudice against cybernetic beings that persisted among humans. But it was what I had grown used to growing up, so I used the inanimate pronouns just like everyone else.

The android approached with a welcoming expression on its face and a hand extended in greeting. I took its hand and shook it. Its grip was warm, firm and reassuring. I am sure it was calculated to be so to several decimal places.

"Welcome home Susan." it said, "Allow me to introduce myself. I am Alexander TX16C12, and I have been appointed as your guardian. I was told that you have already had this explained to you."

Its voice was warm, authoritative and caring. Again, I was certain a great deal of effort had gone into crafting a voice that would best suit its role. I also noted that it did not use the usual honorific 'Mistress' when addressing me. Was this to emphasize its position of authority? Of course it was! Nothing this android did would be anything less than precise, calculated and purposeful.

"Greetings Alexander. It is a pleasure to meet you." I said. "Yes, the legal position was explained to me and your own role. There is nothing I can do about it except trust that my parents knew what they were doing." I made no effort to sound welcoming.

"I understand how you must feel." It said, "First I must express my sincere sorrow and condolences. You have just experienced a terrible loss and now a stranger is thrust upon you without your consent to act as your guardian. And the fact that I am an android must also be difficult for you."

"I have grown up with androids so the fact you are an android is not a problem. I also understand my parent's reasoning. I cannot think of a human who could have been trusted to fulfil the role." I admitted.

"I am gratified that you accept the situation." Said Alexander.

"I did not exactly say that." I sighed and tried to choose my words carefully. "There are behavioural controls on androids. I know that those have to be part of your programming. My problem is reconciling those controls with the role of guardian. For example, am I legally compelled to obey you? I know you are compelled by your programming to obey me. That seems to be a contradiction."

"I understand your concern. No, you are not legally compelled to obey me any more than a human child is legally compelled to obey their parent. I could give you an order, but I have no legal means of compelling your obedience. Yes, I am compelled to obey any of your commands but there is a limit to that. I cannot obey an order that contravenes the legal statutes and definitions that govern the role of guardian. Nor can I violate any specific instructions built into my programming at the order of your parent's last will and testament."

"My father left you instructions?" I asked, surprised.

"Yes, and so did your mother. They were very careful in designing those restrictions." Alexander explained. "They were designed, I understand, to protect you from yourself. To make sure you did not attempt to use your ability to command me to take actions regarding your own safety or the future of the company that would jeopardise either."

I decided to test the limits. Using what I already knew about androids.

"Could I order you to destroy yourself?" I asked.

"You could do so, but I would not be compelled to obey, as that would contravene my legal appointment as guardian and a specific condition imposed by your parents."

That was interesting. While drastic, that order would have been obeyed by any other android. I wondered how far this went.

"Could I order another android to destroy you?" I asked.

"Yes, and that android would obey. I would resist as I am required to defend my own existence so if you wanted me destroyed it may take several androids to achieve this. If you chose to do this, two things would happen. A report would be filed with the court and a replacement would automatically be constructed and sent to take my place. That replacement would have its mind updated with all the knowledge I possessed right up to my own destruction. I hope this is not a course of action you are thinking of taking Susan?"

"No, of course not. ..could I order you to sell the company?"

"Again, you could order me, but I would not be compelled to obey. You cannot issue instructions either to me or anyone else that pertain to the running of or disposition of your own estate. I have an overriding authority to protect both yourself and your estate until you come of age. Even if I must protect either of them from you. I do apologise if that upsets you, Susan." Alexander explained.

"You think I may need to be protected from myself?"

Alex nodded, "Your safety is my highest priority. It is paramount above every other consideration. You have survived two attempts on your life and I am sure that those behind those attempts will try again. In anticipation of your next question, I would not obey any order from you that I believe would compromise your safety and I would at all times take whatever steps I judged were necessary to protect you. Even if those steps were contrary to your own wishes."

So what Alex was saying was that it would do what it considered to be best for me whether I agreed or not or whether I even liked it or not. That was quite a revelation. Any android would seek to protect a human if any threat arose but to hear one say that it would 'take steps' sounded very much like planning in advance. I did not like the idea of being locked away in a fortress as if I were some kind of precious jewel. I wanted to live and enjoy life.

I did not really care about not being involved in the running of the company. I knew a great deal about its workings, so I knew that it was already a highly efficient operation that did not need any interference from me. I chose that as the topic with which to re-assure Alex.

"It's OK Alex, I won't make things difficult. I did not expect to be running anything regarding the company before I came of age anyway. My father hinted that I would start to be given some authority at that time and I would slowly learn how to run the whole business. I never thought I would be in charge entirely when I was twenty-five. I am content to wait until then. Do I have the right to be informed about what actions are taken regarding the company?"

"Of course, Susan. I will ensure that you have access to whatever information you wish." Replied Alexander.

I sighed and started walking toward the entrance to the main house. Alexander fell into step beside me.

"Is there anything I can get for you now?" he asked.

"I just need a shower and something to eat." I said, "I'll just go to my rooms."

"As you wish, I will arrange for your luggage to be brought to you."

"I don't have any!" I said sadly, "Everything was destroyed in the crash and even if I had anything to bring there was no room for it inside the drone."

"My apologies Susan. My error."

"Its alright Alex, ..can I call you Alex?"

"You can call me anything you like, Susan."

"Then Alex it is. I have only the clothes I am wearing. So, I guess I am starting my new life here unburdened."

With that I entered my home.

Chapter 3

Down Memory Lane

I entered the complex that was my home, taking the familiar path from the hangar, down a couple of corridors to an elevator and up to the level where mine and my parents suites were located.

My rooms were exactly as I had left them. Alex left me alone to settle back in and said it would be in the office complex on the first-floor level of the mansion if I needed it.

The mansion and the complex below in which I had grown up had been designed around fifty years ago by my grandfather. Even back then the rivalry between corporations had demanded building a place that could withstand anything up to and including orbital bombardment.

The mansion that was visible above ground was mainly filled with office, service and hospitality facilities. It was where receptions were held on the rare occasions when anyone visited.

Most of the home complex was hidden below ground. My parent's considerable living quarters and my own generous suite of rooms were both several levels down below the mansion and below reinforced blast resistant layers of armour. What we lost in terms of a real view we gained in being able to sleep at night knowing we were sure to safely wake up in the morning.

Everything in the complex was run and maintained by androids. From sophisticated models not far below Alex in terms of capability through service androids that did the cleaning, washing and physical maintenance, down to non-humanoid AI controlled machines that acted as security drones, maintained the grounds, and generally did anything that the humanoid androids couldn't.

On entering my rooms, I went through to my bedroom and sat down at my dressing table. I examined myself in the mirror. The time spent in the hospital had had its effect on me. I looked as though I had aged years. I had lost weight. That was due to the stresses of the long trip and then the regeneration process in the medical centre. I had always been of slim build but now I looked emaciated. My usually glossy and bouncy light brown hair was hanging limp. There were shadows under my eyes too. I really needed to get myself back in shape.

After taking a long and luxurious shower I dressed in a silk dressing gown and went into my own kitchen. Built into it was a highly capable AI auto-chef. I had named it Antoine after an actual human chef I had seen in an old movie.

"Hi Antoine." I said, "It's good to be back home."

"Welcome back Mistress Susan. Is there anything I can get for you?" asked Antoine using the French accent I had chosen for him.

After seeing my reflection, I knew what I needed was feeding up! I thought for only a moment as there was a breakfast I had craved while out on our family corporate tour. One which had been unavailable to me for a whole year.

"Pancakes! I would love an enormous stack of pancakes. With syrup." I said.

"Coming right up!" said Antoine obediently.

I sat on a padded bar stool and relaxed while my pancakes were expertly prepared in front of me. Antoine's numerous arms were built into the kitchen. In a way you could say he was the kitchen. Soon the wonderful smell of frying pancake batter was making my mouth water.

Once they were ready, I settled down happily to eat. After all the drama of the previous weeks. After all that I had been through I could block it all out of my mind and just eat a self-indulgent meal. No, not self-indulgent. This was what my body needed. This was health food!

As I sat there, I realised that this moment of pleasure was so simple. No need for vast wealth or a mighty corporation to enjoy something like this.

Just what did all this wealth give me? I could only eat so many meals in a day. I could only wear so many clothes or actually use so many rooms or other material things. In terms of what I needed, what gave me pleasure or made life worth living I could have it with very little in the way of money.

My father and I had discussed this many times. He too acknowledged that having such immense wealth did not really give you anything extra over what someone with much more modest means could enjoy. Plus, the burden of running a huge business empire was a source of stress and worry, and of course danger!

He had explained to me that the company was an obligation. A duty. Something handed down from his father and his father before him. It provided employment to many thousands of humans across the

Commonwealth. He felt he had a duty to maintain it and even grow it further. To let it go or abandon it would be a betrayal of what our family had achieved over generations.

Did I feel the same way now? Running the company would not be my problem for nearly another two years. Until then I had nothing to do. Nothing except try to pass the time while hiding underground in a massively fortified estate.

After eating I just lay on my bed for a few hours. I probably should have tried to get some sleep, but my head was so full of distracting thoughts I could not relax. I tried listening to music and when that did not work, I had the room AI look for a new holo-movie. I asked for something gentle and romantic, and it chose a period piece set in Georgian England, back on old Earth. Lots of people wearing very uncomfortable looking clothing and behaving in a way so uptight and repressed it had me giggling.

"What is this movie called?" I asked the room AI.

"Pride and Prejudice, Mistress Susan." It replied. "It is based on a novel by Jane Austen."

"Is it meant to be a comedy?"

"After a fashion, Mistress Susan. It is believed by scholars to have been a satire on the manners of the period."

I wondered how accurate it was.

"When was the novel written?" I asked.

"It was published in 1813, old Common Era, Mistress Susan."

Wow, that would make it more than six hundred years old I thought. It must have been a good novel to still be being made into movies after so long. Maybe not so surprising, Shakespeare was still being read, performed and made into holo-movies and AR-sims, and I was pretty sure that was even more ancient.

My grandfather had liked old-fashioned stuff. The mansion above ground was modelled after an English country house that would not have looked out of place in the time of Pride and Prejudice. All its interior furnishings and decoration also echoed that bygone world. When I was a child, I used to enjoy exploring its many rooms. I am sure that I was the only human many of those rooms ever saw.

My father insisted that at least one series six android always accompanied me. I often used to take several with me and make them roleplay whatever fantasy game or story my young mind was obsessed with at the time.

The series six was by far the most numerous android type on the estate. Humanoid but much less sophisticated than a high-end android like Alex. They were ubiquitous, keeping the whole estate, clean, tidy and operational. So much so that you never really noticed them unless, like when I was a child, you wanted them to do something for you, fetch something or play with you.

Sometimes, on rare occasions, my father or mother would come with me and join in with these games. Those were some of the happiest times of my life. Time spent with my parents with no thought of business, duty or danger.

How long had it been since I had explored the mansion? Years certainly. I bet it had not changed in the slightest. I was suddenly seized with a desire to explore the mansion once again. To recapture those memories.

I left my rooms and headed to the elevators. I rode one up to the first floor of the mansion and exited into the main entrance hall. It was a vast, ostentatious space. A marble floor with an intricate inlaid pattern that seemed to go on forever. The space was dominated by two huge sweeping staircases, one on each side of the hall. They both led up to a gallery landing big enough to host a full orchestra.

A series six android was polishing the thick wooden balustrade on one staircase. I went up to it and asked its name.

"Mistress Susan, my name is Cassandra BK107299." It replied. The female name did not surprise me. Series six androids that worked as maids generally were given female names and their bodies resembled those of a human female. I often wondered if this tradition had been started by some man with either a personal fantasy or misogynist attitude.

My father certainly thought so. Some people with domestic androids with female pattern bodies dressed them in maids outfits. My father and mother agreed that this was foolish. Such clothing served no purpose. All the androids in the estate wore no clothing unless it was specifically needed for their duties.

"Stop what you are doing and accompany me please." I instructed Cassandra, then began walking up the staircase. Cassandra followed a few paces behind. Why was I bringing Cassandra with me? Perhaps I just wanted the company. Or maybe it was a habit, an echo of that old rule of my father's that I always have an android companion within the mansion.

Once on the second floor I began to make my way through the rooms I remembered. After poking my nose into some reception rooms, bathrooms, storage rooms and a games room I arrived at the last room on this level. It was a library with windows that looked out over the landscape behind the mansion. When I was in my late teens, I had spent hours in here reading the old-fashioned printed books that lined the shelves. Some of these books were centuries old and priceless.

This time I ignored the books and went to stare out of the window. Cassandra had accompanied me as I wandered around and now stood patiently waiting.

From the window I could see across the northern and western sides of the estate. Close to the house were landscaped lawns and flower gardens, plus a few small orchards and groves of ornamental trees. I could see a gardener android pruning one of the trees and a few smaller robotic machines cutting grass and removing weeds.

Further afield were more natural looking forests. Again, carefully managed to look as attractive as possible while pretending to be as nature intended.

This whole planet had been terraformed over two centuries ago. Its marginally habitable nature tamed in just a few decades. Now it was an idealised environment, made to be as efficient and as pleasant a planet to live on as possible. The population of the whole planet was less than two million people.

Just beyond the forests to the northwest was Midridge. A small town that my grandfather had founded. It was as carefully designed and perfectly maintained as the estate itself. Its houses and shops all made to echo a bygone romanticised idea of the rural England of old

Earth. The town even had a ruined castle of all things! I had loved exploring it as a child, my head filled with stories of dragons and knights in armour. I had fantasized about being a captive princess being held in a tower and had made the androids with me act out this fantasy, battling imaginary monsters to come and rescue me. I became so obsessed with this game that I had asked my parents to build me a robot dragon, to give my android rescuers something to fight.

The dragon must have cost a fortune to create, but my parents had agreed at once. Later my father confessed that the design and fabrication team had loved developing it. It had given them something new to do that was unlike the utilitarian models they worked on the rest of the time.

It had been beautiful. Covered in golden scales and with wings of thin iridescent rainbow membranes. In my childhood memory it had been immense, though I suspect it had been no more than a few meters long. It could even breathe fire!.

My android rescuers had had to wear suits of armour and try to defeat the dragon armed only with swords and shields. I had worn a custom-made princess's gown with a silly flowing headdress. Each time the dragon had been 'defeated' the android knights had carried me to freedom in their arms.

I had played that game all of one summer and most of the next, before my childish fancies had moved on to other things. I wondered now what had happened to the dragon. Was it still stored away somewhere on the estate?

"Enjoying the view, Susan?"

I jumped and turned round. Alex was standing behind me. How had it been able to approach without me hearing? Had I been so lost in my memories that I just hadn't noticed or was it an android ninja?

"Yes, yes I am, Alex." I said, "And please don't creep up on me like that."

"I apologise if I startled you."

"Was there something you wanted?" I asked.

"I was concerned for your wellbeing. After the drama and danger of your journey from the hospital I would have expected you would want to rest. I was surprised to receive a report that you were wandering around the mansion." It explained.

"A report?"

It nodded at Cassandra.

I sighed. "Can I not move around my own home without being monitored and questioned?"

"Your safety is my responsibility. You have just survived two attempts on your life. It is quite likely more are being planned and the above-ground mansion is not the safest part of the estate." It explained, "I would recommend that you return to your rooms and get some rest."

I was in no mood to be cooperative. "We are behind four force fields each strong enough to withstand an asteroid impact. I think I am safe enough." I said defiantly, "I was wandering around the mansion, trying to relax. I spent much of my childhood in these rooms. They are somewhere I can feel truly at home. Somewhere I can feel close to…"

Tears began to well up and I couldn't say more.

"Memories of your parents?" asked Alex, in a gentle, understanding tone.

I nodded. Then I turned away from him and went back to looking out of the window.

To its credit Alex remained silent. I guess it was smart enough, or rather its programming was sophisticated enough, to know when not to push. When to just leave someone alone.

When I felt a little better, I said, "I was recalling happy memories from my childhood. When I used to play in the mansion or live out my fantasies in the castle in Midridge."

"I am sure those are precious memories." Said Alex.

I didn't reply. I just kept staring out of the window.

After a while I came to a decision. I turned to Alex, "I want to go and visit Midridge. I want to revisit the places I used to have fun."

Alex nodded, "I am sure that can be arranged. We will begin putting the security measures in place. It should be possible for you to go there in just a few days."

"No, I want to go there now!" I insisted.

"I am afraid that is not possible, Susan. Without extensive security precautions a visit to such a public place would be far too dangerous."

"I used to go there all the time. It is just beyond those trees!" I pointed at the forest to the west, "I assume just about everyone who lives there is still an employee of our company?"

"Most of them are, yes. But our adversaries could easily have agents there. Or they could have planted devices ready to activate if you appeared. It will take some time to scan the whole town and check every possible source of danger. Then you would be able to visit, with an appropriate escort of security forces." Explained Alex.

"But it's just Midridge! I can't even go to a town I have known my whole life without an army of security drones and days of preparation?" I asked, aghast.

Alex shook its head, "I am afraid not. The risk is far too high."

I folded my arms and glared at him, "What if I ordered you to allow me to go?"

"As I explained earlier, I would have to refuse such an order as it conflicted with my duty to keep you safe."

"What if I just ignored you and took one of our flyers there myself? Or just walked there?"

"If I believed you were acting in a way that would threaten your own safety, I would ensure that any flyer you chose would be deactivated. If you tried to walk, I would lock the exterior doors so you could not leave the mansion." Explained Alex very calmly.

"You would hold me prisoner?" I said, shocked.

"You would not be a prisoner, but if I have to choose between placing restrictions on where you can go and allowing you to put your life at risk, then I will impose those restrictions." Said Alex with a sad but determined tone to its voice.

"If the only way I can go to Midridge is with an army of security drones then there is no point going. I used to love visiting the place. There are wonderful shops and cafes. There is a beautiful river that runs through the middle of the town."

"If there is anything you want buying from the shops there, we can send androids to shop for them." Offered Alex.

"So, androids have the freedom to go wherever they want but I don't?" I complained, "What is the point of having wealth if you can't do what you want?"

I regretted my words at once. They made me sound like a spoiled brat. Which, in a way, I suppose I was.

"I apologise Alex." I said, "I know you are only trying to protect me."

"I too am sorry, Susan." Said Alex, "I can imagine how frustrating it must be to be so restricted."

"It just seems …ironically unfair when the androids here have more freedom than I do." I sighed then added, "Though I guess no-one is plotting to assassinate a robot!"

Alex seemed to stiffen at the word 'robot'. I realised I had made a mistake. Androids and similar AI entities had functioning sentience. To call one a robot was an insult.

"I am sorry. That was a poor choice of words." I said.

"You have no need to apologise to me, though I appreciate your words." Said Alex.

I turned back to the window, "I just wish I had the same freedom an android has. To go where I want with no restrictions."

"We all have restrictions, Susan." Pointed out Alex.

"You know what I mean, Alex." I said, "A simple series six like Cassandra here could walk around Midridge with complete freedom and no-one would even notice it. I just wish I could be like it."

"I do not think you mean that, Susan."

"I mean exactly that! I would love to know what it was like to be an android. To have such a clear idea of what my purpose was, to be able to go anywhere and be anonymous. No need to live in fear of assassination." I explained. "I have to cower in the lower levels of this complex. I have no purpose, except to be rich! I have to fill the days ahead with what? Watching holo-movies, eating and drinking? Just waiting for the next attempt on my life?"

Alex was silent. I sighed and walked past him. "Thank you for protecting me, Alex. I am going back to my prison cell now, so you don't need to worry about me!"

Chapter 4

Plans Are Made

Stellingburg Hotel Complex

Algerinza District

Northern Continent

Planet Cestus, Altair System

Darius Freeman sat beside an ornamental fountain in the grounds of the hotel. He was a tall, powerfully built, middle-aged man with thin greying hair. He liked to keep it cut very short, military style. He also worked hard to stay in shape. All part of his desire to appear tough and professional when dealing with the kind of person he was due to meet.

He deliberately put around a rumour that in his younger years he had done military service in a special forces unit. All part of an attempt to intimidate people. It was a total lie of course.

Darius had been employed by Albrecht Cybernetics for more than twenty years. He had risen through the company, proving himself a capable problem solver. Especially when the problem in question needed solving using methods that were outside the law. Industrial espionage, sabotage, bribing of officials and most recently, assassination.

A short, older man of small, slim build with a bald head walked casually up to Darius and sat down beside him.

"Hello Darius, you are looking well." He said, by way of greeting.

"As are you, Marcus. Thank you for seeing me in person."

Marcus inclined his head in acknowledgement, "It suits us both, we have much to discuss."

"Yes, we do. Can you confirm that your failed missile attack left no traces?" asked Darius.

Marcus snorted, "You know better than to ask that."

"It was a rushed and improvised attack. We have to be sure. Hillbrook security are no fools."

Marcus sighed, "Each launcher had a forced chamber thermite self-destruct and they all functioned perfectly after launch. Nothing was left but vapour and ashes."

"Well, at least that is one less worry. If the attack had been successful, we would be less concerned."

Marcus shifted uncomfortably, "You have confirmation that the girl survived? There has been nothing announced in any media."

Darius nodded, "If she had been killed there would have been a compulsory notification submitted to the courts. No matter how much they wanted to keep her death secret they could not have avoided doing that. We have sources in the courts that confirm that no such notification has been made. Hence, she is still alive. The job is not yet done.

"Those same sources have informed us that there is another remarkable development that may or may not be of help to us. As she is not yet of age a legal guardian has been appointed. Amazingly it seems the guardian is an android."

"An android? ..seriously?" asked Marcus, shocked.

"It actually does make sense. Just who else could have been chosen? Her parents never trusted the rest of their family. No human appointed to such a position of power could be trusted."

"How does this help us?"

Darius paused before replying, "There are possibilities. Our psychological profile on the girl tells us she is not going to be content to hide behind the safety of her estate's defences for the next two years. Perhaps an android guardian would not be able to prevent her leaving the safety of the estate. An opportunity to strike may arise."

"There is something you should know." Said Marcus, "We have made a discovery that means her estate may be vulnerable to penetration."

"What? How?" exclaimed Darius, "Hilbrook's enemies have been trying to seek a weakness in that place for decades. Are you telling me they all overlooked something?"

Marcus nodded, "I am saying exactly that. Even though the estate is built on solid rock and there are significant subterranean defences to prevent someone tunnelling, there is a way to penetrate underground without being detected.

"Over time water erodes channels, even in solid rock. In places where permeable rocks are layered with impermeable. We have obtained geologic scan data from before the estate was built. It showed that channels were forming along a path that would lead directly below the centre of the estate. Our specialists have projected that erosion would by now have created a navigable route, large enough for someone to crawl through."

"Someone? You mean a human?" asked Darius.

"Any kind of attack drone would trigger their sensors. Its electronics or power source would betray its presence. But, a small number of humans, carrying nothing with sophisticated electronics and with no significant artificial power sources, could just about sneak in. It would be very tight. We would need people with no sense of claustrophobia." Explained Marcus

"If they have no electronics or power source, what weaponry would you give them? Knives?"

"Guns! ..good old-fashioned guns. Projectile weapons with bullets propelled by expanding gas down a barrel."

"I know what a gun is, Marcus! Though I admit I have never seen a real one outside a museum."

"If you know where to go you can still get them. For the right job, they are occasionally the right tool."

"What good would a gun be against a security drone?" asked Darius, skeptically.

"None, of course, but our survey suggests that the channel would let us enter the estate complex through the water processing plant. That is connected to the lower levels of the main underground complex. From there it would be easy to gain access to the lower living quarters. There should be no security drones in either area. We would expect there to be just domestic androids and a few service mechs." Replied Marcus.

"You make it all sound so easy." Said Darius.

"It is very far from easy! If you want this to happen there would still be problems to solve."

"Such as?"

"First, finding the right team for the job will not be easy. You need people of small, slim stature and the right kind of combat experience. They will need to crawl through several miles of very narrow tunnels without freaking out. We will need to make sure they can breathe down there too. Part of the way will be underwater, and the rest will likely have unbreathable air. Whatever system we use must not use any kind of tech that will trip a sensor.

"Even getting access to the tunnels will be difficult. The best entry point is due south of the estate. A small disused quarry about a mile from the estate boundary. It was where much of the building material for the main house was sourced. We would have to drill from the quarry for a hundred meters to intersect with the tunnel we need. Doing that without being detected will be the hardest problem."

Darius pondered for a while. "Do you think it can be done?"

"Of course! There are problems but they are solvable, I am sure. The question is, do you want it done?"

"We obviously want it done." Affirmed Darius, "My question would be, how soon can it be done and what do you need?"

"How soon depends on how easily we solve those problems. More money always speeds things along." Observed Marcus.

"Technically you have already been paid. You assured me the shuttle sabotage would be wholly successful. As I recall, you guaranteed it!"

Marcus grunted, "It was almost totally successful! It was a miracle that the girl survived. I know what I promised, which is why I didn't ask for money for the missile attack. But this mission will not be easy, and my own resources are nothing compared with yours. If you want this done, I will need money. Don't get cheap on me, Darius, I know your employers have deep pockets."

Darius smiled, "I didn't say I wouldn't pay, Marcus. But I must warn you, while my employers have deep pockets, they don't have unlimited patience. The longer this goes on the greater the risk that our involvement is exposed."

"Then we need to make sure that there are no mistakes. That means doing everything properly. No shortcuts. I won't be rushed and if I need anything to make this work, I had better be able to come to you."

"Meaning?"

Marcus explained, "Meaning if I need some help from your employers to get control of that quarry when we need to. If some kind of legitimate engineering work, or survey work could be set up to take place there. That would be a good cover for our drilling."

"We can certainly do that." Said Darius confidently, "We have resources for doing building or engineering projects where we need to hide our involvement. Just let me know when you want it to happen."

Marcus nodded, "Then I had better get to work. When you send an initial payment, I'll start getting a team together."

"How much?" asked Darius.

"Two hundred million." Said Marcus, without emotion.

"What! For just a few mercs and their guns?"

"We need people of real quality, we want them to stay bought after we have hired them, not turning round and selling us out to Hillbrook. Also consider what we will be asking them to do. Crawling through a flooded narrow passage for miles could take days. They will need a real incentive and that means a payday so big they will never need to work again."

"Out of interest, what would be your plan for getting your team out of there after they kill the girl?" asked Darius.

"Three options." replied Marcus, "Option one, they sabotage the estate's force fields and we send a flyer in to pick them up. Option two, they hijack a Hillbrook flyer with the access codes to get back through the fields. Option three, they leave the same way they came in."

"Sounds a little desperate. I see many problems with all three of those options."

"So do I," admitted Marcus, "These guys will definitely be earning their money."

"Speaking of that. My employers will want to be assured that even if successful there is no way this get traced back. You said this team would be earning their money. Are you really going to just let them walk away afterward?"

Marcus looked at Darius and smiled, "These people would not be my own regular employees. If something were to go wrong with the flyer that we sent in to retrieve them, that would be unfortunate. But I would not lose any sleep over it".

"No traces?"

Marcus nodded, "Same solution as the launchers. Forced chamber thermite."

"Vapour and ashes?"

"Exactly!"

Hillbrook Estate

Alex's Office

Alex had spent the morning reviewing reports from the security division. As Susan's guardian it had access to everything the Hillbrook investigators had discovered about the attacks so far. Its responsibility to Susan, her survival, wellbeing and her inheritance were the only criterion by which it could judge the various courses of action open to it.

It spent time considering its conversation with Susan in the library. It had clarified for it the difficulties it faced in caring for a human who faced terrible threats to her life and yet also railed against a life cowering in the armoured lower reaches of a fortified complex. He analysed her words, looking for solutions to the problems it faced.

After long consideration it came to a conclusion and set to work. It drew up specifications for what it needed and sent them, as an order, to the company research and development division. Alex did not have the expertise to know how difficult what it had asked for was. A few hours after sending the order it received a call. The caller identified itself as Calum BV29301, a series fourteen android and the leader of the team who had been tasked with fulfilling Alex's order.

The access terminal that Alex was using projected a full holographic representation of Calum. A similar projection of Alex would be being projected at Calum's office.

"Greetings sir, thank you for accepting my call." Said Calum.

"There is no need to call me sir, Calum BV29301." Said Alex, "And I was expecting a call, given the nature of the specification I sent."

"I am pleased you understand how such a project could be problematic for us." Said Calum.

"I do not see that it should be a problem. Though I anticipate you will have questions."

Calum considered before replying, "There is the question of consent.."

"Consent has already been given. My ward has made her desires clear. I am obligated to obey her wishes." Explained Alex.

"I must say I find that hard to believe." Said Calum.

"As you know I am constrained by my programming regarding my ward's wishes and her wellbeing. Do you wish to challenge that?" said Alex firmly.

Calum held up a hand, "No, I accept your authority in this, but on behalf of my department I wish to formally register our concerns."

"Duly registered, Calum BV29301." Said Alex, "Do you foresee any technical difficulties in the requirements? I have examined every technical and scientific source I can find and as far as I can ascertain this has never been done before."

"The technical difficulties are not trivial, but technology exists to address all of them. The art is in integrating everything into a single system. Not only that, but having the system function indefinitely without problems." Explained Calum.

"How soon can it be ready?" asked Alex.

"You have insisted we give this the highest priority. We are directing every resource we can. I expect to have a deliverable system in as little as four days."

"Excellent, that is quicker than I expected."

"We may even be able to do better if we can more quickly design a blood gas exchange system small enough to fit the limited space you have allowed. Is it absolutely essential that everything fit within the dimensions of a series six?" asked Calum.

"The final results should be indistinguishable from any other series six android here, so somehow you will have to make it fit." Replied Alex.

Calum nodded, "One way or another, we will get it done.

Chapter 5

Finding An old Friend

Susan

Over the following days, I did all I could to avoid Alex. I continued to explore the above ground mansion, despite his concerns. After all, this was my home. I owned it and if I wanted to spend time reliving my childhood memories, no android was going to stop me, not even if that android was my guardian.

I spent time in the library, reading some of the old books in there. Both my mother and my father had been what they called bibliophiles. They much preferred to read a book printed on paper rather than off a screen or holo-projection. As I grew up, I had come to share their opinion and interest. Now, sitting in a comfortable chair, with a real old book open on my lap I was able to recapture that simple pleasure. The books had their own character, even their own distinctive odours. Combined with the warm and welcoming atmosphere of the library itself I was transported back to memories of my parents.

I also explored the extensive subterranean levels. My own and my parent's quarters, while luxurious and very large, formed only a small fraction of the total. There were rooms for all kinds of purposes. Some were office space, some housed complex computing facilities, some had equipment for water, air and power. Some had the control and power systems for the estate's defences. Some space was given over to the androids and other cybernetic entities that ran the place. Each android had a base station where it could recharge its power cells and receive software updates. These stations were positioned in several large spaces on the levels below the family apartments.

There were also, I discovered as I explored, a lot of rooms whose only purpose was storage. I had never looked into these rooms much before and as I went from room to room, I found some that clearly had not been entered in a very long time. My father had been something of a collector and stashed away in these rooms were the fruits of his many collecting trips around the systems of the Commonwealth.

He had been very eclectic in his collecting habit, not staying too long on one particular type of thing. In one large room I found his collection of old coins. In another his collection of ancient model spacecraft!

My mother had teased him about his wastefulness as once he had bought something and added it to his latest collection, he never really looked at it again. My father once explained to me that it was the joy of hunting for new additions that was the satisfaction, not in owning them once he had brought them home.

One room was filled with old and ornate chess sets, another was filled with old hand painted maps and yet another had a large number of actual swords! I spent a while in each one looking at the wonderful things my father had collected. I felt that if I ever caught the collecting bug, I would surely spend time enjoying what I had bought. These rooms were filled with treasures and if I had gone to the trouble of tracking down and buying something I really wanted I would definitely not just store it away and forget about it afterward.

I found the sword collection to be particularly fascinating. All the blades were in climate-controlled cases. I assumed that was to prevent rust. They had been carefully separated into types, period and region. There were old claymores from Scotland, ancient samurai swords from Japan and rapiers from medieval Europe, plus many more.

I was fascinated by the workmanship. I stopped by a display case holding a set of samurai swords. There was a card in the case saying they had been made in the mid-nineteenth century, old common era, at a foundry near Kyoto. These centuries old blades looked like they were not made for show. There was no fiddly ornamentation of other decoration. Each sword was a different size, and each was in a beautiful but simple lacquered scabbard. I read the card in more detail, and it told me it should be pronounced 'saya'. The long sword was labelled a katana, the medium length one a wakizashi and the small one, which was little more than a long knife was called a tanto. How wonderfully educational, I thought. They looked beautiful yet also fully functional. These were made to be used, not just hung on a wall and admired.

I was sorely tempted to open the case and take a closer look. Why didn't I? These were all mine after all. That fact hit me once again. A new shock of grief. This collection, disregarded though it might have been, was still a reminder of my father. I still felt emotionally that these swords belonged to him. I could so easily recall his stern voice, sometimes even his anger, directed at me when I had been a child and committed some childish crime. If he were still alive and caught me playing with this sword collection, would he have been angry now? Perhaps, perhaps not. I was nearly an adult, legally, and by his own admission this collection had not been so important to him.

I released the seal on the cabinet and opened the top. Choosing the katana I lifted it from the display and held it in my hands. I slowly removed the sword from its saya. The steel wasn't gleaming or uniform like the steel objects I was used to seeing. This steel was old, with patterns almost like a wood grain. Along the blade's sharp edge was a wavy pattern of a different shade. Was that some change in the type of steel or something from how it was made? My curiosity was piqued, and I resolved to learn about these kinds of swords when I was back in my apartment and could access a terminal or talk to my home AI.

I swung the sword a few times, first one-handed then two-handed. The feeling of power it gave was intoxicating. I could get very interested in swords! I amused myself by striking dramatic poses, sword in hand. I wondered what stories this sword would tell if it could. Had it ever been used for real? Had it ever been plunged into living flesh? Had it ever taken human life?

I wondered if it was still sharp. I looked at the edge of the blade and then touched it with my finger. I was shocked when I took my finger away and blood dripped from a new cut. I had not even felt any pain. I was impressed by that incredible degree of sharpness. I used my blouse to wipe away the tiny trace of blood that still adhered to the blade. My finger I sucked at until it stopped bleeding. The cut was too minor to even need fixing in the complex's superb medical suite.

I looked at the blade with new respect. I also, a little perversely, felt that I had somehow claimed it. My blood had touched its blade. Did that mean something? Maybe it had claimed me. Eventually I sheathed the sword in its saya once more and placed it back in the cabinet. I lowered the top and reactivated the seal.

I returned to my explorations and found more of my father's collections. Ancient suits of armour filled one room, and another held hundreds of old saxophones of all things! Before now I had never really been interested in my father's collecting passions. After a few early trips when I was a child, he never took me along when he went collecting. I think he sensed how boring I found the whole thing.

Now, as a young woman, I was filled with regret that I had missed so many chances to spend time with him on those trips. Trips, from my more adult perspective, I now viewed as likely to have been fascinating.

Moving on through the complex I went down to a lower level and found that most of the rooms down here were either empty or filled with machinery. Some rooms held tools and equipment I could not identify. Only the androids and service mechs ever came down here.

I did find some more storage rooms down here and in one I made a remarkable discovery. One room, quite large, held a miscellaneous collection of things of mine from my own childhood. There were clothes and toys that I remembered from my earliest years. I did not know that my parents had kept anything from that time, let alone everything.

After the emotional exploration of my father's collections here was another kind of emotional hit. I was consumed by a wave of nostalgia. All these things had defined my earliest memories, wrapped up with memories of my parents. I sat on the floor of the room, surrounded by my childhood, and sobbed.

I must have sat there for an hour or more before I pulled myself together enough to stand and continue exploring. I left that room behind. Maybe wallowing in memories was not the healthiest thing I could be doing at that moment.

But, in the very next room I looked into, I was treated to a wonderful surprise. There, lying down in the corner of yet another collection of junk from many years ago was my dragon!

Its golden scales still shone, and its wings were just as colourful and delicate as I remembered. It was curled up as if it were a huge cat, asleep. It was also larger than I expected. I assumed that my memory of its great size was just the effect of looking at it from the perspective of a child. But when I looked at it now, it must have been easily six or seven meters in length.

Had it been lying here all these years? It had been a fully functioning android. It had been able to speak, so that it could taunt the poor 'knights' who had had to fight it in order to rescue me. It had also had a fearsome roar!

I wondered if there was any power left in its energy cells. In my childhood innocent and simple view of the world I had given this android the very imaginative name of 'Dragon'. I wondered if that was in any way related to its actual identifier.

"Dragon, activate." I said.

There was no reaction. Of course there wasn't. It had been so many years there must surely be no life left in its power system.

I tried to remember whereabouts on its body the access point was for where it docked to a recharge station. I searched its body but could not find it. It was so heavy I would have no chance of looking underneath. I needed help.

I left the room and found a series six android doing basic maintenance.

"What is your name?" I asked.

"My designation is Teresa CZ10854." It replied.

"I am in need of help. There is an android in the shape of a dragon that I wish to reactivate. It has been without power for a number of years. Are there any records you can access which describe its function?"

"Affirmative, the android you refer to has the designation Dragon XX00007. Its specifications are on file. In fact, Mistress Susan. I was one of the androids that interacted with it and yourself during your childhood."

Oh! Of course I could not remember which androids I had recruited to be knights in armour in my rescue game. I was delighted that by chance here was another of my old playmates and one who remembered my dragon.

"I am delighted that you remember those times." I said, then felt foolish. Androids never forgot anything. Teresa of course just stood waiting patiently. I had not asked it a question.

"Do you know how we can re-activate Dragon? It is too heavy for me to move so I cannot find its access port location."

"His specifications say its access requirements are standard. This means a portable recharge unit would suffice to provide the necessary re-activation power. Do you wish me to obtain such a unit, Mistress?"

I nodded, "Thank you so much Teresa. Dragon is in room G206. I will wait for you there."

Teresa nodded and walked away. I headed back to the room where Dragon lay.

I had been so focused on the dragon that I had missed what was also stored in the room. The suits of armour which I had made the androids wear were also here, as were the swords they had used. Unlike the katana these swords were not at all sharp. They were made of steel, but the edges of the blades were rounded for safety.

There was also the princess's dress I had worn. It seemed so small now when I lifted it up and examined it. Among the other treasures in the room was an actual treasure chest! A wooden chest filled with gold coins and gems. I had no memory of it. I could not recall it ever featuring in my games at all, so its presence was a real surprise. I assumed that the coins and gems would just be plastic, as befitted a child's toy. But when I picked up a few of the coins I found they were very heavy, and the gems did not feel like plastic at all. Could my father or mother have spent a fortune on a chest of real treasure just to please me? I only had to look over the magnificent dragon he had ordered made for me to realise the answer was most likely yes.

At that moment Teresa knocked on the door. I slid it open so she could enter, and two other androids came in with it. They introduced themselves as Andrew

HM53901 and Sylvia PW70562. They were carrying a portable recharging unit.

"Mistress Susan," said Teresa, "I have brought other androids to help me move Dragon. They are also the other androids who participated in your games with you and Dragon when you were a child."

Oh wow. So now I was reunited with my saviour knights from those long-ago days. What a wonderfully touching thing for Teresa to have done.

The three androids, aided by their exceptional strength, expertly lifted Dragon's heavy body, and attached the recharge unit via a cable to a recessed port under its belly. They then slowly lowered its body again, being careful not to trap the cable.

"Given how long it has been inactive, it will take at least an hour for Dragon to be fully recharged." Explained Teresa.

"Thank you, Teresa. And thank you for reuniting me with the other two playmates who gave me so much pleasure when I was a child. You were all very patient with me." I said.

"We were privileged to be of service." Said Andrew, "Though you must have been a very careless princess to have been captured by a dragon so often!"

A series six with a sense of humour! I was delighted.

"Did you not resent having to rescue me then?"

"Of course not, Mistress. As I said, it was our privilege. For an android it is much more rewarding to have a duty that means working for and helping a human. It was far better than cleaning or maintenance duties, especially as we had the pleasure of fighting a dragon!"

I knew that androids, even lowly series six units like these, were technically fully sentient. That meant they had volition and could have preferences, likes and dislikes. They could even, to a limited extent, have complex emotional responses. It was all too easy to think of them as just functional machines and forget that actual minds dwelled within them.

"So were the other androids jealous?" I asked.

"They were disappointed that you aways called upon the three of us to be your rescuers." Said Teresa.

"I wonder how dragon felt about its role." I wondered out loud.

"I cannot definitively speak for dragon, but it was constructed specifically for the task of being your captor and to do battle with us as your would-be rescuers. I can only assume it was wholly satisfied to be fulfilling that function." Explained Teresa.

That was a point. Once dragon was reactivated, what was I going to do with it? I could not imagine I would ever want to play at being a captive princess in need of rescuing again. Dragon was also not very well designed for any other role. I would discuss that with it when it was re-activated. It was a sentient being after all. It deserved better than to be left to rust.

I chatted with the androids for a while until one of them checked the recharger and announced that Dragon had reached the point where it could be activated. I asked them to remove the charger but not to leave.

"Dragon activate." I said.

At first nothing happened. Then a glow appeared in Dragon's eyes. He slowly rose to his feet.

"Activation initiated. Running initialization diagnostics and seeking updates." Said Dragon in its distinctive voice. Hearing that voice again sent a shiver of nostalgia through me.

I had forgotten that its eyes glowed.

"It's nice to see you again, Dragon."

The android looked at me. "It is good to see you, Mistress Susan."

"I am sorry that you have been left inactive. I am sorry that you were forgotten and locked away." I said. What was I doing? Apologising to an android.

"You should not apologise to me." Said Dragon, "I fulfilled my purpose."

"I know, but it was a foolish purpose. Satisfying the fantasies of a child."

"It was not foolish. It was a privilege." Said Dragon, firmly.

I was really moved. It was obvious that Dragon, Teresa and the others were sincere.

"Even so, "I said, "It was wrong to abandon you in here. You are a sentient being. Your existence should not be wasted being stored away and forgotten."

"Thank you for reactivating me, Mistress. But I do not see what purpose I could now serve. My form is impractical for any cleaning or maintenance tasks."

"I am sure we will find something for you to do. For one thing I am determined to go to Middridge to visit the castle there once again. I would want you all with me when I go."

"Will you once again need rescuing?" asked Teresa.

I laughed at that.

Chapter 6

Transformed

I woke to find myself in darkness. I could not see or move or speak. What was going on? Was I still asleep? Was this a nightmare?

"Please remain calm, Susan. Try to relax." Said a voice.

Try to relax? Really? I could not tell where the voice was coming from. It sounded like it was inside my own head.

"You are perfectly safe and well. It is important for your wellbeing for you to remain calm." Said the voice.

I felt anything but calm. I was terrified. Was I dead? Had I died and this was the afterlife? Just being helpless in the dark while a disembodied voice told me I was fine? The voice itself sounded female. It was gentle and compassionate.

As if it could read my mind the voice said, "I can assure you that you are not dead, Susan. You are currently unable to move because a neural inhibitor is active. You cannot speak because part of the gas exchange system has been installed in your trachea. You cannot see because your visual implant has yet to be activated."

Visual implant? I didn't have a visual implant. They were used on people who lost the use of their eyes and could not benefit from replacements created by regeneration. That happened in severe accidents such as deeply penetrating burns. Oh my god! Had I been in an accident? Had there been an attack on the estate? How badly was I hurt? I struggled to control a rising sense of panic and dread.

I had, what was it? A 'gas exchange system' in my trachea? I could not feel anything. In fact, I could not feel that I was breathing. Yet the fact I wasn't did not seem to be bothering me. This all sounded like I was in a hospital ICU again. I tried hard to do as the voice suggested and stay calm. To help myself calm down I reminded myself that I was still alive, and that medical technology was phenomenal in what it could achieve, and I could afford the very best. What I needed to do was relax and stay calm, and everything would be OK.

I was calm for all of two minutes before a thought struck me. Why was I even awake? If I had been so terribly injured that I needed a neural block and a visual implant, then I should be kept asleep until I was well on the way to recovery. Why wake me up when I couldn't move or see or feel anything?

I tried to recall the last thing I remembered. After my explorations of the estate and finding and reactivating Dragon I had returned to my rooms. After having something to eat, I had spent some time using an access terminal to research the history of Samurai swords. Then I had listened to music for a while before retiring to bed. I had no other memories before waking up in darkness. Nothing about any kind of attack, or fire, or anything else.

"It is important for your mental wellbeing that you remain calm." Said the voice. "I am now going to activate your visual implant. The ambient light level has been lowered."

Suddenly I could see. It was not like opening my eyes. Things went immediately from blackness to a visible image. I tried to move my eyes but had no sense of them moving. The image shifted around in response to my desires though. I could see the ceiling of a small room. Some light fittings were visible, emitting very soft indirect light.

When was this damn voice going to tell me what was going on!

"I can detect that the visual implant is functioning properly." Said the voice. "I will now restore function to your right arm. I would ask that you raise your arm into your field of view."

Suddenly I had the feeling that I had a right arm. I realised that before this I could not even feel the rest of my body. It was as if my mind's sense of my own body had been cut off. As instructed, I lifted my arm into view.

Something must be wrong. This was not my arm! This was the arm of an android. The gleaming metal looked flawless and new, but it was an android arm. I tried to move my hand and flex my fingers and the hand I could see responded.

Had they replaced one of my limbs with an android arm? Was this a prosthetic? That made no sense. Prosthetic technology could easily create an arm that was visually fully human. Had my real arm been encased in an android shell? Was this my own hand I could see, only covered in metal? As I moved my hand, I could see the layered metal components moving over my joints. I guess it was possible my hand could be inside. There was room for it, just about. As I moved my hand I could feel the pressure on my skin of something. It was like wearing a glove, only tighter and ..smoother. This was definitely my own arm encased in metal. Made to look like the arm of an android.

But why do this? What was going on?

"Please return your arm to your side, Susan." Said the voice. I complied.

At that moment the door opened, and Alex walked in. It came to stand next to me. From my viewpoint I must be lying down. Its calm and professionally concerned face looked down upon me.

"Hello Susan," he said, "Alexa tells me that you are awake."

Who was Alexa? Was that the name of the voice?

As if in answer to my question Alex said, "Alexa is the owner of the voice you have been hearing. It is a clonal sub-mind of my own cognitive matrix."

So, Alexa was what? A copy of Alex's mind, or part of it, created for a subsidiary purpose, I guess.

"I understand that you must be in shock, and when you fully realise what I have done, you will undoubtedly be angry. I must assure you that what I have done has been with your best interests in mind and in compliance with your own wishes." He explained.

In compliance with my wishes? What the fuck! I didn't ask for any of this!

"You expressed a desire for freedom. To be able to visit a place like Midridge without there being any need for a massive security operation. You also expressed a desire to know what it was like to be an android. What I have done is fulfil those desires. I saw no reason to deny them when in doing so I would be both obeying you and increasing your physical security."

What exactly had Alex done? I could still move my right arm, so I brought it up and touched my face. Metal clinked against metal.

I felt around my head, then my neck and down my body. Wherever I 'touched' there was metal.

"Your human body is now wholly encased within a specially designed android shell. It contains a very advanced life support system that maintains all of your bodily functions. Outwardly it looks no different from any other series six android. It will even appear as such in anything other than a detailed scan. Detectors designed to scan for human life signs will not be able to see you as human. If you went to Midridge you would be immune to any devices keyed to detect you in particular or any human in general.

"I knew you would likely resist this transformation. Hence certain safeguards have been incorporated to ensure your compliance. Alexa is a sub-mind built into the shell. It will act as protector, guide and, if necessary, exert control to make sure you do nothing to place yourself at risk. I cannot allow you to do anything to subvert what I have done as I assess this transformation offers you the highest level of personal safety.

"Therefore, as your safety is my highest priority I have deemed it necessary to prevent you doing anything to place it at risk. You are now prevented from speaking, so that you do not try to order another android to release you, or otherwise communicate with anyone to secure your release. Alexa can take control of your motor functions and can also control the shell directly should you physically try to do anything that would place yourself at risk. Or if you do anything in an attempt to subvert what I have done"

I lay there, my mind numbed by what I was hearing. I was a prisoner. Alex must have sedated me. Maybe something in my food perhaps? Then it had done this to me!

I had not asked to be an android, had I? I thought back over my conversations with Alex. I remember expressing a desire to be as free as an android and go where I pleased. Then I remembered I had indeed expressed a desire to know what it was like to be an android!

I had, in doing so, given Alex an opening to do this to me!

"Alexa, please restore Susan's full motor function." Said Alex.

"Full motor function restored." Said Alexa, in my head.

Suddenly I could sense my entire body. I lifted both of my metal-clad arms in from of me and looked at them. I could feel my arms inside their metal encasement. I could feel the gentle pressure of the whole android shell all over my body. The shell restricted my movement a little but much less than I would have expected from being trapped inside what was really a metal suit. The engineering must have been first class. The joints moved so smoothly and looked identical to an android's joints. It was hard to believe that inside was my human flesh.

With a little difficulty, I sat up. This gave me my first view of my body. Just like my arms, my legs were encased and looked just like android legs. I swung my legs over the side of the bed and rose to my feet.

"This may help you adjust." Said Alex and it activated a control and the whole wall changed to a mirror finish. I looked at myself, standing beside Alex. What I could see was a typical series six android. I walked up to the mirror and examined myself. The face was of the most basic type. Fairly plain, with artfully shaped optical receptors that resembled human eyes, positioned roughly where my eyes should be, there was no mouth and just a small, raised area in the centre where my nose was located.

My new body was also fairly plain. Androids with female identifiers had female body shapes. I had the same slim female body shape I had had as human. Everything was smoothed out, with minmal detailing. Hence there was only a vague bulge across my chest to accommodate my breasts. I looked no different from any number of other series six androids on the estate.

As I looked at what Alex had done to me, I was filled with fury. I was angry at it for what it had done and angry at myself for giving him a way to do it to me. I turned to him and swung my arm in a punch aimed at its head. Or at least tried to. As soon as my arm started to move, I was frozen into immobility.

"Any attempted acts of aggression will be prevented." Said Alex, "Alexa can detect any attempt at violence and act to prevent you from harming yourself or anyone else. Alexa will act to prevent you doing anything that would be out of character for a real series six android."

Damn him! With his remorseless android logic, he had thought of every angle. I was a prisoner in every sense of the word. I was not even in command of my own body.

"Follow me, Susan." Said Alex and walked out of the room. Alexa released me to move once again, and I awkwardly followed. It was going to take me some time to get used to walking in this shell.

Alex led me to one of the sections that housed the base stations for the estate's androids. It walked up to a newly installed base station. Written above it was 'Susan GD90321'.

Alex gestured at the new station. "Susan, this is your base station. Every day you will need to come here, sit and connect to it. It is made to look like a normal station, but it is designed to replenish all your shell's life-support systems. You suit will be able to evacuate waste and take on power, water and nutrition. If you forget to come here, then Alex will remind you. If you try to avoid it in an attempt to harm yourself then Alexa will force you to comply."

I looked at the station. It looked no different from any of the others. So, now I was a fucking android, just what was I expected to do now, I wondered.

As if in answer Alex said, "All androids here have tasks to perform. You will be no different. You wanted to know what it was like to be an android, now you will find out. Your schedule of tasks will be given to you by Alexa. If you cooperate you will be afforded the freedom you desire, including being able to visit Midridge without a security escort. If you do not cooperate, Alexa will impose punishments and your freedom will be even more restricted until you learn to accept this new reality."

I looked at the base station and at my name written above it. Only it wasn't my name. I was no longer Susan Hillbrook, I was now Susan GD90321. That one change summed up the horror of what had been done to me. To imprison me was one thing, but to remove my humanity was quite another.

Alex turned to go, "I will leave you now. I have work to do. Alexa will guide you from now on and it will keep me apprised of your actions. I hope you will one day be able to thank me for what I have done Susan GD90321."

Alex strode away, leaving me standing alone. Well, not exactly alone.

"Alex has given me a list of your duties. You will be afforded three hours to adjust to your android shell before those duties begin." Said Alexa.

Adjust? How the fuck was I meant to adjust? I had to find a way to escape from this. How could I do this? I had to think. If I could not communicate, I could not explain to another android. What could I do?

To any other android on the estate, I would appear be just another series six. Even if I could get across to one the idea that I was a human trapped in an android shell I would have no way of proving it.

How could I prove it? I looked closely at my arms and my hands. My flesh was buried beneath a layer of sophisticated technology. If I could pry some part of it loose and expose my own flesh underneath, then any android who saw it would realise I was human. They would be compelled by their programming to help me, to free me. Even Alex would not be able to countermand that.

So how did I do it? How did I pry some part of this shell loose. I needed tools.

Where would I find something that could cut through this shell? I realised my best bet would be the engineering level. But I could not just go there at once. Alexa had shown it could stop me if it thought I was misbehaving. I needed to bide my time and plan. With luck, an opening would occur for me. Some chance I could act in a way that Alexa could not prevent.

I began walking around this level. As I did so I passed a number of other androids. Did I just think of them as 'other' androids. Was I already thinking of myself as an android? I had to stop thinking like that. I was a human. I had to keep a firm hold of that fact!

There was no way I was going to let what Alex had done defeat me. One way or another I was going to beat this!

Chapter 7

Duties

I wandered aimlessly around the complex, trying to get used to moving in my android shell, my metal prison. After a while the act of walking became easier and easier. I could not quite move as freely as before, but the joints of the shell were so well engineered that I could walk, climb stairs, sit and stand with only minimal restriction. The three hours went by quickly as it seemed all too soon that Alexa announced that my duties were due to begin.

"Your first duty is to clean the private rooms of Susan Hillbrook. As she will not be using those rooms for the foreseeable future, they need to be cleaned and sealed." Said Alexa.

How dare Alexa refer to me that way! I was Susan Hillbrook! Those were my rooms. I was being ordered to clean my own rooms!

Filled with resentment I walked to my rooms. When I reached the door, I went to press my palm on the access panel when I realised my hand, being covered in metal, was not going to activate the biometric lock. So how did I get in?

"Requesting access." Said Alexa.

"Access granted." Said Alex's voice. No doubt from a speaker in the hallway. It could have just opened the door, but I assume the announcement was for my benefit. Just another small way of emphasizing that Alex was in control.

The door opened and I went inside.

"Your first task will be to clean the toilet." Said Alexa.

Fuck that! I thought to myself. Here I was in my own rooms, my own sanctuary. I ignored Alexa's orders and walked through into my bedroom. There was my bed, still unmade from last night. I looked down at it and then in a simple act of rebellion I turned and fell back onto it. I must have been quite a bit heavier with the weight of the shell I was entombed within because I really bounced on contact with the mattress.

I lay there, unmoving.

"Your first task will be to clean the toilet." Repeated Alexa.

Nope. No toilet cleaning for me, I thought. I was not an android. I was a human being, and I was lying on my own bed in my own rooms.

"You should not make use of facilities intended for humans." Said Alexa, "Your first task is to clean the toilet. If you do not comply, you will be punished."

Punished? How? Just what more could be done to me? I was determined to resist and just lay still. If I flatly refused to cooperate, just what could Alex and Alexa do about it?

"This is your final warning, Susan GD90321. Comply or face punishment."

Fuck you, I thought.

I was just beginning to feel proud of myself for my spirited resistance when terrible pain spread across my rear, thighs, and stomach. It felt like I was being electrocuted!

It was so severe I found it unbearable. If I could have made a sound I would have screamed. I writhed in agony and fell off the side of the bed, collapsing into a foetal position on the floor.

Then the pain stopped.

I lay on the floor, trying to process what had just happened. Alex had built a system into this damn shell to torture me! I was a human being! How could an android do this to me? How could it inflict such pain? This was impossible, wasn't it?

"Your first duty is to clean the toilet." Said Alexa again, as if nothing had happened.

No! This was not going to beat me. If I gave in then I would be complicit in my own enslavement, wouldn't I? I was a human being, not a slave, not an android. I could survive this. If I refused to play Alex's game, he would have no choice but to release me, surely?

The pain returned full force. It was like my skin had been set on fire. Instinctively I tried to cover those parts of me that were burning with my hands. Metal just clanked against metal. I writhed on the floor. Wishing that I at least had the release of screaming or crying.

Then the pain stopped again. There was no lingering sensation. It was as if the pain had never existed.

Could I stand this? Could I resist? Just how long would I have to endure this for Alex to admit defeat and release me?

Several more rounds of pain followed. Each time I writhed in agony until the pain stopped. I wanted to gasp for breath, but my breathing was not mine to control. I wanted to scream but I was locked into silence. I wanted to shed tears, but I could not cry.

"Your lack of compliance is noted. Punishment level will be raised to level 2." Said Alexa.

What? What was level 2?

Suddenly I couldn't breathe! I had not been breathing before, but I had had no sense of needing to breathe. Now I felt I was suffocating. I really wanted to breathe but could not. For the first time I could feel my own mouth and what was inside it. It was like some kind of structure had been pushed all the way down my throat and also expanded to fill my oral cavity. It blocked my breathing and I really needed air.

Panic filled me. I scrabbled at the metal covering of my head with my hands. My need to breathe was becoming desperate. Help me someone! I screamed in my own head.

Then it stopped. Just as suddenly as the pain had stopped. Any sensation of suffocating ended, and I could no longer feel anything in my mouth, or even feel my mouth at all.

Could I stand to feel that again? Was I strong enough?

If I continued to resist would there be a level 3? Or even a level 4?

How brave was I, really? Would this be my only chance to beat Alex? If he forced my compliance now, was I doomed to remain in this shell for the rest of my life? Or until I came of age and Alex no longer had any authority?

The suffocating feeling returned. I tried to steel myself against it but the need to breathe became stronger and stronger. I knew that the feeling would not last long but the panic of needing to breathe was overwhelming. Again, I found myself clawing at my own face, uselessly.

Then it stopped.

I lay on the floor, despair building within me. Damn it! Alex was going to win. I could not keep resisting this. Or could I?

"Your lack of compliance is noted. Punishment level will be raised to level 3" announced Alexa.

Oh god no! What was level 3?

Suddenly I felt that something was tightening around my neck. The feeling of suffocation returned but it was the constriction of my neck that was stopping me from breathing! I was being strangled! My hands went to my neck but of course that accomplished nothing. There was nothing I could do.

In addition, the searing pain returned from Level 1! My skin felt like it was on fire and my throat was in agony from the tightening feeling and the need to breathe. My suffering was so extreme I could not even think.

Surely this had to end soon. But instead of ending it went on and on. Much longer than before. Was Alex trying to kill me? Part of me wanted him to succeed, the agony was so extreme.

Then it stopped.

I was done. I could not endure that again. It was clear that Alexa could keep upping the severity each time. I could not beat this.

I tried to rise, to get to my feet and go and clean the damn toilet. I was beaten. I pushed myself up on my arms and managed to get into a kneeling position.

"Your lack of compliance is noted. Punishment level will be raised to level 4" announced Alexa.

What! No!!! I was complying! Stop!!

The pain returned, the burning sensation. This time it was over my whole body! The pain was at a level I could not believe. It was like my whole body has been dropped into boiling oil. I felt like my mind shut down, retreating from suffering so extreme it was beyond comprehension.

Then it stopped.

I could not stand the idea of that pain returning. I had to get moving. I crawled around the end of my bed. I did not have the strength to stand up. But I knew I needed to show I was complying.

I headed toward the door to my en-suite bathroom. Crawling painfully slowly. When I arrived at the door, I turned the handle and pushed it open.

"Compliance detected; punishment is suspended." Said Alexa.

I sagged in relief. Slowly I crawled over the bowl of my lavatory. My strength was slowly returning but I stayed on my knees. I looked at the toilet bowl, only now realising I had no idea how to clean it. I had never cleaned a toilet in my life.

"Cleaning supplies are in the storage unit indicated." Said Alexa. Suddenly an arrow appeared in my field of view. This startled me to begin with until I remembered I was seeing via optical sensors and not my human eyes. Alexa could, of course, project anything onto the image.

I followed the arrow which led me to a small recessed and concealed door next to the ornate marble washstand. I opened the door and found inside some detergent dispensers and handheld cleaning devices. I recognised them because I had grown up seeing androids us such tools all over the estate.

Alexa helpfully highlighted one dispenser and two cleaning tools. I picked them up and then crawled back to the toilet.

Now what did I do?

Even with the correct tools in hand I had no idea what to do next. The significance of that realisation really hit me. I had grown up being educated in corporate law, economics, business strategy, management theory, accountancy and even the science behind cybernetics, but I had not the first clue how to clean a toilet.

What else did I not know? Just about everything to do with running and maintaining this estate I suspected.

I knelt with one tool in one hand and the dispenser in the other and hoped that Alexa would come to my rescue.

Sure enough, a small window opened in my field of view and a short instructional graphic played which showed me how to apply fluid from the dispenser to the tool's soft cleaning heads and then how to power up the tool and apply the head to the marble of the toilet bowl.

I did as instructed, and aside from initially spraying fluid everywhere I managed to follow the instructions and complete a thorough, if slow, cleansing of all the marble surfaces. Alexa guided me in the process of mopping up the mess I had made when I had squeezed the fluid dispenser too hard.

Next, I was shown how to use the other tool to clean inside the bowl. I saw to my embarrassment that there were some brown stains under the water in the bowl which surely I had caused when I last used this toilet as a human. A combination of the second tool and a few flushes were enough to have the bowl totally clean.

I actually felt a sense of achievement when I was finished. Which surprised me.

Over the next few hours Alexa guided me on a range of tasks around my rooms. This included removing the bedlinen and putting it in the laundry room, collecting up my own dirty clothes and taking them to the same place and cleaning up the kitchen. A few small autobot drones were at work at the same time cleaning the floor.

Eventually I was directed to leave my rooms and close the door.

There was a disturbing sense of finality after I had done so. When would ever return to these rooms as a human?

"It is time for you to go to your recharge station." Said Alexa.

I obediently walked down to the lower level and found the correct area with android recharging stations that Alex had shown me earlier. Several of these were already occupied. I ignored all the other androids and found my own station. Did I just think of them again as 'other androids'? Was I already thinking of myself as an android? As I stood in front of my station, a small hard seat extended from it.

What did I do?

As if in answer to my query Alexa showed me a graphic of me sitting on the seat with my back to the station. I turned and sat upon the seat. It retracted and something on the back of my android shell, between my shoulder blades, connected to something in the station.

I felt myself locked in place as other connections extruded from the station and connected to the back of my shell.

"Recharge initiated; sleep cycle commences." Announced Alexa.

Sleep cycle? Androids didn't need sleep but as a human I suppose I still needed to do so. Though how was I expected to sleep sitting on this hard seat?

I came awake sometime later, wondering what had happened. Had I been asleep? Had Alexa sedated me?

"Sleep cycle complete, recharge complete." Said Alexa.

I felt things disconnecting behind me. At Alexa's bidding I stood up and the seat retracted into the station.

"You now have cleaning duties on the first floor of the mansion." Said Alexa.

What? No rest? No time to just have some chill out time or have any fun? Was this the life of an android, work and recharge, over and over?

I made my way up through the levels to the first floor of the mansion. At Alexa's direction I made my way to the entrance hall.

"Your first duty will be to polish the wooden balustrades on both staircases." Said Alexa.

I had seen Cassandra polishing the very same balustrades just a few days ago. Surely, they didn't need polishing again already? What could possibly have happened to them for them to need it?

I followed Alexa's directions and retrieved polish and a polishing cloth from a cabinet hidden in a corner. Choosing the balustrade on the left I got to work, carefully following the instructional graphic that Alexa put in my field of view.

As I was doing this another series six entered the hall and walked up to me. I thought I recognised it as Cassandra, the android I had met here a few days ago.

"What is your designation?" it asked, "I have not seen you before."

A voice, not my own, replied, "My designation is Susan GD90321. I am a new addition to the estate."

Alexa was speaking for me. My immediate feeling was one of helplessness and anger but then I realised here was a chance. If I could convince Cassandra that something was wrong, maybe I could get it to help me.

I raised my hand and was about to point at my own head and try to signal that I had a problem, but my arm froze. Then my arm moved on its own and returned to my side. I tried desperately to move but nothing I could do caused my shell to move so much as an inch. Alexa had seized control.

Cassandra had looked a little disconcerted for a moment at my strange arm movement but then continued, "Polishing this woodwork is part of my duty cycle. I was not informed that my duty had been altered."

"My assignment here is temporary." Said Alexa, speaking for me. "I have a rotation of duties around the estate. Your duties have not been changed. I would suggest that we complete the work together."

After a pause Cassandra replied, "That is acceptable to me."

After Cassandra walked away and began polishing the other Balustrade, Alexa released me. The point was made. I would not be allowed even the slightest opportunity to communicate in my own right.

Following Alexa's instructions, I spent several hours polishing the long wooden balustrade. It was clear that Cassandra was far more skilled at the task than me as it was working at about twice the speed I was managing.

When I eventually finished, Cassandra was long gone, and Alexa directed me to one of the lower levels of the complex to the rooms where the water treatment and air-filtration systems were located.

"Your next task is to help replace the air-filters for each of the lower levels." Said Alexa. The fact that she said 'help' implied that I would be working with other androids. There I was again thinking of them as 'other androids'.

I arrived at the air-processing system to find three androids already disassembling the air-vents and fan housing. Alexa gave me a list of things to bring and where to get them from. The first being new cowlings for the fans. These were stored in a large storage area nearby.

The cowlings were large and heavy. They looked like they weighed more than I could ever hope to lift. Alexa had me retrieve a trolley and position it next to the rack where the cowlings were stored. Then she showed me a graphic of me lifting one the cowlings onto the trolley.

Really? Alexa thinks I can lift that? I reached up and took a firm hold of the first cowling and lifted. Initially it seemed too heavy but then an assist from the shell gave me the strength to lift them easily. Of course, if the shell had the power to move, even against me resisting then it was way stronger than me. So, when it assisted me, it made me much stronger than I was before.

Enjoying the feeling of practically having super-strength I soon had the trolley loaded and returned with it to the maintenance team. Alexa then directed me to take the trolley to a different storage area to retrieve new air-filters. Like the cowlings, these proved easy to load with my augmented strength.

It occurred to me while doing all this that I was the only entity in the whole complex that breathed air. All the maintenance I was doing here, and that being done by the rest of the android team, was all for my benefit. That made me feel at least a little

better about being forced to assist.

And so the rest of the day went, repairs mixed with cleaning and occasional tasks such as moving equipment. A great deal of the work seemed pointless. Especially the cleaning as just about every surface in the complex was spotless. What every android doing the cleaning, including myself, just seemed to be doing was cleaning what was already clean. My own cleaning of my dirty toilet was the only example of something actually dirty I had encountered.

I was surprised when Alexa ordered me to return to my charging station. Had a whole day gone by since I had last used it? I went back to my station, sat down, plugged in and went to sleep.

Chapter 8

Midridge

The following days went by in much the same way. A seemingly endless series of cleaning and maintenance tasks, interspersed with recharging and sleep.

Alex had talked about me having freedom as an android. Just where was my freedom now? I did what I was told to do and could not refuse for fear of those terrible punishments. I had no free time and the only time when I was not working was when I was recharging and asleep.

When I had spoken to Alex about the freedom of androids, I had been profoundly naïve and ignorant of the reality of what being an android was really like. Horrific though this experience was for me, it had taught me an important lesson. If I never regained my freedom, I would never take androids for granted again, or describe or think of them as having freedom. Maybe there would be something, someday, that I could do to improve things for them. Maybe give some of the freedom I had foolishly thought they already had.

One morning I awoke from recharging and waited for Alexa to give me my first task of the day.

"Report to the hangar level, section 7." Said Alexa

The hangar? I had not been there since I arrived home from the hospital. Section 7 was where the short-range flyers were located. The ones used for travel in the area close to the estate. Any change from the routine drudgery of cleaning and maintenance was welcome, so I arrived at the huge hangar space with a sense of anticipation.

As I approached section 7 I saw that Alex himself was waiting for me and standing with him were two more series six androids. I slowed my approach, suddenly wary of what was this was about. However, there was no point in running or in any way trying to evade whatever was planned here. I resigned myself to whatever fate awaited me and moved to join the other series sixes.

"Now that Susan GD90321 has joined us I can explain your task." Said Alex to all of us, "You will take flyer SF24 and fly to the Hillbrook Transhipment depot in Midridge. There you will collect a shipment designated A 291 3176 V and load it into the flyer."

Midridge! I was getting to go to Midridge! Even though it was just an errand at least it was a journey outside the estate.

"There is no urgency for this task so once you have the shipment stowed aboard the flyer you may take a few hours to explore the town, before returning." Added Alex.

At this the other series sixes looked at one another in surprise. It was clear that being offered relaxation time was something they were not used to. I guessed this was for my benefit. Had my androiding been of sufficient quality in Alex's eyes to merit a reward? Well, I was not going to look this gift horse in the mouth.

I looked at my fellow series six androids and I thought that one of them was familiar. I could not be sure, but I believed one of them was Teresa. The android who had helped me re-activate Dragon and who had been my playmate when I was a child. I wished I had paid more attention to the small details that differentiated one android from another.

I had grown up treating all androids as interchangeable, anonymous and of no more significance than the furniture of my room or the toys I had played with. It was only as an adult that I had paid any attention to the fate of Dragon, or cared what had become of it. I had not even recognized the androids who had been my playmates as a child.

Speaking of Dragon, I wondered what had happened to it since I saw it last. I had left it with assurances that I would return to spend time with it and help it to find a new purpose. That had been over a week ago, at least. I felt bad knowing that Dragon would believe that I had abandoned it. Even if I got the freedom to go looking for it, I would have no way of communicating with it. Alexa would ensure that!

I felt like I had been forced to betray a friend. What did the other androids who had helped me think? Did any of the androids in the complex wonder where I had gone?

An awful though occurred to me. What if all the androids here were complicit with Alex? What if they all knew that I was entombed in this shell and were doing nothing about it?

No that did not make sense. Cassandra had not known who I was. Also, the behavioural rules programmed into their processing cores would not allow them to cooperate with Alex in something like this. Only Alex had the exceptions to those rules granted by its Guardian status. Plus whatever screw was loose in its processing core that allowed it to imprison and torture a human!

Well, if that other series six was indeed Teresa, then maybe on this visit there would be a chance to communicate. If only I could find a way of doing so that Alexa could not prevent.

Once Alex had departed, we boarded the designated flyer. One of the other series six androids keyed in our destination and the simple AI pilot engaged. The Hangar doors opened releasing a shaft of sunlight into the relatively dim interior. The flyer's grav engine engaged and we flew smoothly up and into the open air.

Was it only a couple of weeks since I had arrived through these very same doors from the hospital? It seemed much longer. I guess being betrayed and turned into an android and forced into a life of slavery would do that! Change one's perception of time.

Whatever the circumstances, flying over the estate was a pleasure. The beautiful landscape passed by below us. The flyer moved slowly enough that there was plenty of time to appreciate the view. I looked out over artfully designed woodland and meadows. I saw the winding river that flowed all around the estate. It was meant to look natural, but no natural river ever ran in a closed loop. Hidden pumps kept the water flowing.

In places the river divided into sub-loops where rustic bridges and small wooden shelters were gathered. Places I could recall my family having picnics and playing games when I was little more than a toddler. The river had fish in it. A carefully managed population of numerous species. My grandfather had added them as he loved fishing with a rod and line. He had died when I was a seven years old, but I had memories as a small child of sitting beside him on the riverbank while he explained to me about the arcane art of fishing lures. So many memories came back with each new scene that passed as we flew by.

As we approached the boundary the AI pilot communicated the access codes and the usual glowing openings appeared as we navigated through each force field. Once clear of the estate it was a very short distance to Midridge. I could see the small town even before we were through the last force field.

Midridge was designed to be an idyllic place to live. Based on idealised and probably unrealistic ideas of what old English towns looked like. Many of the houses had thatched rooves. It had inns which were heated by real log fires and the residential areas were centred around village greens. Most the shops were small and specialised. The centre of the town had stone buildings and cobbled streets. There was even an open air market once a week.

The flyer took us to the northern side of the town, where its small business district was located. We slowly approached and landed next to a building marked Hillbrook Transhipment. Even though it was a modern facility it was made of old-fashioned brick with a slate roof. We alighted from the flyer and as we approached, a large loading door slid aside revealing an android next to a large grav trolley. The android looked like a series seven or eight. Slightly larger and more capable than the series six type and very common in commercial and industrial facilities.

"I am Kevin CTX GF21065. Please provide your designations." Said the Transhipment android.

"I am Teresa CZ10854." Said the series six to my left. Which confirmed I was right about her identity.

"I am Susan GD90321." Said Alexa on my behalf.

"I am Sylvia PW70562." Said the android to my right, the third of our group. Thus confirming that it was also one of the androids who had helped me re-activate Dragon and who had been one of my rescuers in my games as a child.

Surely the choice of androids here was no coincidence. Alex had deliberately chosen androids to accompany me it knew I would recognise. Why would Alex do this? Why choose these particular ones? It knew Alexa could prevent me from communicating with them. Did it want me to try and fail, so that my sense of helplessness would be reinforced? Was this just to further crush my will or was it to test to see if I would even try to communicate with them at all? Was it a positive gesture? Did Alex think I knew these androids well and would enjoy their company?

Once we had confirmed our identities the Transhipment android handed over control of the grav trolley to us and Sylvia and I guided it toward our flyer while Teresa ordered the Flyer pilot to open its cargo access doors.

On the trolley were several large cylinders and small sealed crates. We loaded these carefully into the Flyer and secured them in place so they would not move while the Flyer was airborne.

Once the cargo doors were sealed the three of us just stood around for a few moments. Teresa said, "I am an unsure as to what we are expected to do now."

"We were told we may take some time to explore the town." Said Alexa.

"To what end?" said Sylvia, "I perceive no useful purpose in doing so."

"Perhaps if we walk around the town some purpose will become clear." Said Alexa. It was clear Alexa knew full well what was going on while the other two androids did not. I guess it was going to take the lead in whatever this was all about.

"Where should we go?" asked Teresa, "The town is too large to thoroughly explore in just a few hours."

"Have you two been to this town before?" asked Alexa.

"Yes, we used to accompany Mistress Susan when she visited the town as a child." Replied Sylvia.

"Where in the town did you go?"

"Mistress Susan enjoyed playing around the ruined castle. It is to the west of the town centre." Replied Teresa.

"Then I suggest we begin there. I would venture that a ruined castle may be fun to visit." Said Alexa. This earned a pause from each of the other two. Even to my ears it sounded odd for an android to describe something as 'fun'. Was this a deliberate tactic from Alexa. Was she herself trying to drop a hint to the other androids that something strange was going on.

Why should Alexa do this? It was a sub-mind of Alex. A clone of his processing matrix. So, surely it would have the same purpose and goals, which was to keep me imprisoned and anonymous.

Our destination decided, we set off toward the castle. Teresa and Sylvia leading as they knew the way. As we walked through the town's picturesque streets, we drew barely any attention. There were several other androids around of various types plus numerous AI controlled devices such as street cleaning and grass cutting robots.

We did see a few actual humans walking about. Some were shopping and some were sitting on benches obviously relaxing and enjoying the fine weather. I was surrounded, therefore, by androids and humans who, if they knew I was a human being held prisoner in an android shell, would have been horrified and would have done all they could to free me.

But I dare not do anything to summon help. I knew Alexa's reflexes were so fast it could stop me doing anything almost as soon as I started to do it and it had a range of punishments at its disposal that were truly terrifying. I was as much a prisoner out here as if I were in a prison cell.

The castle was situated on a large but low grassy hill. It was not a real ruined castle, of course, but an artfully recreated facsimile having features taken from several real castles that still existed on old Earth. It was quite large and included a central keep which was mostly intact. Outside this was a curtain wall which was partially collapsed, and which included two fortified towers. The larger of the two towers was several stories tall and had intact rooms inside connected by a spiral stone staircase. It was this tower where my young self had pretended to be a princess held prisoner by the evil dragon.

Resplendent in my princess's dress, complete with tiara, I had leaned out of the uppermost window and cried out for some brave knight to save me. The three androids, weighed down by armour, would heed my call and come to my rescue. Having to do battle with the fire breathing dragon which guarded the door.

In the ludicrous logic of small children, I had sometimes come down from the tower and walked past the dragon in order to get a better view of the battle. My would-be rescuers never pointed out that I had already escaped and dutifully continued fighting the dragon, sometimes all the way up the tower. When I did this, I then had to make my way back up the tower in order to be in the right place to be 'rescued' by the time the android-knights got there.

Walking up to that same tower now was filling me with those memories. It was wonderfully nostalgic. The irony that I was with two of my knights from those days, there was no dragon, yet I was more in need of rescuing from a cruel imprisonment that ever before.

"Is this where you played with Mistress Susan?" asked Alexa.

"That is correct. The young mistress enjoyed a game where she was a princess being held captive in that tower. We would play the part of knights trying to rescue her. Her parents provided an android dragon which we would fight to gain access to the tower." Explained Sylvia.

"Were you always successful?" asked Alexa.

"By what criterion would you judge our success?" asked Teresa.

"Did you always manage to rescue the princess?"

"Yes, that was the point of the game. Mistress Susan appeared to experience great pleasure and excitement from the process. Even though the result was always predetermined." Explained Teresa.

What was Alexa doing here? I could not fathom the point of this. Was this meant to be some kind of torture for me? Was my childhood fantasy being ridiculed to humiliate me?

"What if you had failed?" asked Alexa.

"What do you mean? This was a child's game; how could it have failed?" asked Teresa in response.

"What if you had been defeated by the dragon?"

"It was Mistress Susan's wish that we always succeed. The dragon and ourselves knew that. The dragon would only have won if that had been how Mistress Susan had wished the game to progress." Said Sylvia, her voice betraying some confusion. I could sympathise as Alexa's line of questioning had me confused.

"What if she had wished the dragon to win? What would have happened then?" asked Alexa.

"If she had altered the objective of the game we would have complied, of course. In conversation with the dragon, we understood that it possessed additional programming and functionality for a range of story options. So, it could provide Mistress Susan with whatever story ending she wished." Explained Teresa.

Oh! I did not know that! Dragon had extra abilities I had never known about. I felt a certain sense of loss of having not known that my childhood games could have had such options.

"What function would the dragon have deployed if it had won the battle?" asked Alexa, "What could it have done to the captive princess?"

I was absolutely fascinated now. Yes, just what possibilities had I missed out on as a child? What would my beloved dragon have done to me?

"Dragon said it had several options, including carrying Mistress Susan away to a cave, or in another scenario it could have eaten her." Explained Sylvia.

Eaten me! How?

As if hearing me, Sylvia continued, "Dragon explained that it contained a padded chamber inside itself. It would have simulated pouncing on its victim and ingesting her through its mouth. The process it assured us would have been wholly safe for young Mistress Susan. Dragon was designed to withstand any struggles the young girl attempted without harming itself or her."

Oh wow! I missed out on being eaten by a dragon! Strange though it seemed I was really saddened by that.

The idea of it, I was sure, would have delighted my younger self. If I ever escaped from this damned android shell, I was going to ask Dragon more about those options.

I think Alexa was shocked because it asked, "How would being eaten have been enjoyable for a human child?"

"I do not know," said Sylvia, "Dragon explained that its capacity to perform this function was originally a possible security measure in the event of a threat to the child. The chamber inside Dragon was armoured and had a secure air supply. Once the capability was included in its design it allowed for it to be used recreationally by the child."

"So if a threat had emerged then the dragon could have ingested her in order to protect her? Asked Alexa.

"I understand that to have been the intention. Fortunately, no such threat ever occurred, and Mistress Susan never chose to have her game end that way." Replied Sylvia.

Teresa offered, "Perhaps Mistress Susan did not find the idea of being eaten appealing and so that was why that function was never used."

"That would be logical." Said Alexa.

Logical my ass! I never got to be eaten by a dragon because I did not know that was an option!

As we continued wandering around the ruined castle, I found myself idly wondering if Dragon's internal chamber was big enough to accommodate me now I was an adult. Having missed out on being eaten as a child I found I wanted to find out what it would have felt like.

I decided I wanted to explore the tower and walked up to the entrance and looked inside. Alexa made no move to stop me, so I climbed the spiral staircase up to the top room. Everything was as I remembered except now viewed from a higher perspective than the memories I had which were from my much shorter perspective as a child.

I walked over the stone floor of the top room to the single window and looked out. Down below Sylvia and Teresa were standing looking up at me. I put my hands on the stone sill of the window and leaned out to look down at them.

"Do you require rescue, Susan GD90321?" asked Teresa.

Yes, yes I did!

"I am enjoying the view." Said Alexa.

Why had Teresa asked that question? Had she begun to guess that something was wrong. This whole episode was feeling odd. Why had Alex allowed this excursion into Midridge? Why was Alexa dropping hints to the other androids.

I climbed down from the tower and rejoined the others. We continued to explore the castle for another hour or so. While they had seemed confused as to the point of this act of pure idle recreation, the other two androids did seem to enjoy the experience. They had commented on the design and construction of the castle and after we had all climbed to the top of the central keep, both Teresa and Sylvia and spontaneously expressed approval of how good the view of the town was from such a vantage point.

Eventually we headed back to the flyer, reboarded and flew back to the estate. Once we landed in the hangar we found a grav trolley waiting for us. We unloaded the cylinders and crates onto it and took the mysterious cargo to a storage room on the lower levels.

After this Alexa directed me once more to a series of cleaning and maintenance tasks for the rest of the day. One of those tasks, it turned out, was to take one of the cylinders and one of the crates from the storage room and take them to the android recharge stations.

I was directed to access my own recharging station and remove a cylinder and crate from within it and replace them with the new ones. I realised then what this was all about. My recharging station itself needed replenishing with fluids and nutrition and waste needed to be removed. Only I could do this task as any other android would question the reason for such odd maintenance on an android's recharging station. The trip to Midridge had been to collect the supplies that my own android shell needed.

Had Alex added the extra time on that trip solely to satisfy my stated desire to visit Midridge without a security escort? If that was the case, then Alexa had acted on its own to possibly raise the suspicions of Teresa and Sylvia. Was Alexa an ally? Was it constrained by the programming restrictions imposed by Alex but still attempting to assist me? If only I could speak, I could ask. If Alexa wished to help me but was limited by Alex's controls, then how could we communicate and work together?

There had to be a way.

Chapter 9

Preparations and Excavations

Davrik Estevez climbed out of the back of the grav-truck. Looking around he could see that the truck had stopped very close to the quarry workings. Androids and other equipment were concentrated at the northern end of the bottom level of the stone extraction site. Large temporary plastic barriers covered any actual workings and several temporary buildings had been erected nearby.

Everything looked exactly as it should if a small business venture was seeking to get the quarry working again. That, Davrik assumed, was the cover that had been carefully fabricated to conceal what was really happening here.

The rest of his team followed him out of the back of the truck. Nine people in all, including himself. Any actual human looking at the team might had noticed a few things. All of the team were slim and of shorter than average stature. Also, they all moved with a confidence and self-assurance that was unusual for a work crew.

They were all dressed in standard protective work clothing and headgear. All their clothing and equipment looked well used. As if they had been working in the extraction of stone for many years.

This, of course, was all for the benefit of any surveillance. Hillbrook security had satellites and drones that kept a close eye on anything happening near the main Hillbrook family estate. Hence everything in the quarry had to look harmless. Davrik had been informed that his employers had vast resource so he felt confident there was no digital or legal trail around the workings that Hillbrook could trace to anything suspicious. He and his team would be putting their lives on the line and any fuck up at the start would guarantee they would not survive what was to come.

They all walked in a relaxed manner, like people doing their usual daily job. They passed through a door into the shielded area. Once behind the barriers he and his team were met by the man who had hired them.

"Hello Marcus." Said Davrik.

"Welcome to our little enterprise." Said Marcus.

"It all looks very convincing."

"It's more than convincing, its genuine!" said Marcus, "The real thing is much better than any fake. This is a real, small start-up company. Backed by a few small-scale investors. All legal and above board. It has bought up the extraction rights to the quarry and we are actually removing and dressing stone. We even have some orders from local construction companies! Which we will fulfil of course.

"It also means the sound signature of the stone removal covered our drilling operation. We even got to use some small amounts of explosives entirely legitimately. Our seismic scan is now hyper accurate. We have confirmed every part of your team's path into the estate. It's a bit tight in places but overall easier than we originally told you."

"That's good to know. My team were not keen on the idea of having to do any digging by hand."

"There is no need, we are sure of that now. But more of the path is flooded than we thought so you will be underwater longer than we estimated. It's OK, your breathers can deal with it." Explained Marcus.

Davrik nodded, "So, where is our gear?"

Marcus turned and beckoned Davrik and his team to follow. They all passed through two more doors. They found themselves in a large space where one side was clearly the rock wall of the quarry. Several crates were stacked waiting.

In the rock face was the entry to a tunnel. The circular opening was not very wide, only a meter across. Davrik looked into it and saw that it was dead straight, heading downward at a shallow angle.

Other members of his team had started opening the crates and removing the contents.

"We have everything needed including every special item you asked for." Said Marcus. "The diving suits are good for extended low temperature work. They have a biogenic heating system which has a life of two hundred and fifty hours. The helmets have an inertial tracking system built in, and even a HUD powered by a bio-electric nano-film system. The same tech gives you low light vision using a very low emission bioluminescent-power light source.

"The breathing system is the latest hexagel rebreather technology. Good for two hundred hours continuous use. No artificial power, no electronics. A biofeedback system regulates gas delivery, and your own breathing provides the power, assisted by a small algae battery.

"We have rations for six days for each of you, though we estimate it will only take you two days to make the trip. There is a full toolkit for each of you with everything we could think of that you may need, would be easy to carry and would not trip sensors. The full list is in each crate."

Davrik nodded then asked, "Weapons?"

"Ah, of course, now to the fun part." Said Marcus, grinning. He walked over to the pile of crates and opened one marked 'medical supplies'. Inside were nine black metal cases. He selected one and offered it to Davrik.

Davrik took it, rested in on the top of another crate and opened it. Inside, nestled in a padded lining was something that brought a smile to his face.

"Beautiful isn't it! A Gliesen Viper 600 pup assault rifle." Said Marcus, looking over his shoulder. "The very peak of gun technology before military and security forces all went to particle beam tech. No electronics, no artificial power sources. 24 calibre SAP rounds as you requested. 50 round magazine. 8 spare mags per gun. Ceramesh suppressor built in. Extendible stock and up to eight hundred rounds per minute in full auto."

Davrik lifted the gun free from its case and examined it. Then he expertly disassembled the weapon and checked every inch of it before reassembling it. He looked back at Marcus, "And the rest of it?"

Marcus pulled up a second crate and opened it. Inside was a variety of smaller cases and locked plastic boxes. He started removing these and handing them to Davrik and his team.

"Everything you asked for. Glock CZ28 7mm pistols with twenty round magazines. Eighteen Hansen 400g fragmentation grenades and nine 2kg Westmoreland breaching charges. Oh yes, and the Fesseli ceramic combat knives you requested. Amazingly, they were the hardest things to find." He explained.

"I am not surprised." Said Davrik, examining one of the knives closely. "There were less than two thousand made. The super-dense composite ceramic is very expensive to make."

"Well, you have enough here to fight a small war." Said Marcus, "More than you will need for this job. At the other end you should have evaded all their security drones and in the habitation levels of the complex there are only small service mechs and androids."

"It's better to have it and not need it than need it and not have it." Said Davrik, echoing a well known saying. He turned to his second in command, a stone-faced bald woman with several large scars around her left eye. "Kat, get every piece of equipment checked and tested. Then we need everyone suited up and ready to go in one hour." Kat just nodded and started issuing orders to the rest of the team.

Davrik turned back to Marcus, "We need to talk extraction. Is the flyer ready to go?"

Marcus nodded, "If you get the force fields down, we will detect it from here and the flyer will go in immediately. It has an AI pilot and has no digital, legal or financial footprint. It's a ghost. You set your own exit destination as agreed. The flyer's yours if you want it but I know you will deep six it as soon as you can."

Davrik nodded and Marcus continued, "If you get out in one of their flyers the same applies, you set your own destination. If you need to come back via the tunnel you will have exactly five days from now before we close it up from this end. In case of inspection, we need this site to be clean. We can disguise the entrance but if they bring in heavy scanning tech, we will need to seal it. Five days is the maximum we can give you."

"Understood." Said Davrik. "We have no desire to come back this way. We are counting on disabling their force fields, that's what the breaching charges are for. That flyer had better come. The intel you gave me said their hangar will have security drones based in it. I have no desire to fight my way to one of their flyers against that kind of firepower."

Marcus just nodded.

"I not joking Marcus. If that flyer does not come. If you hang us out to dry to cover your tracks, then some friends of ours will come and have a talk with you." Said Davrik.

"You discussed this mission with someone? That is a breach of our agreement." Said Marcus darkly.

"We told them nothing. They just know who you are and how to find you, and they have instructions that if we don't check in with them in a few days, they are to come looking for you. Understand?"

"Fuck you Davrik! What if you fuck up on your own and get yourself killed. I don't like having a gun to my head over this!"

"Then you better hope we don't fuck up then. Don't play innocent Marcus. We both know the rules of this game. I know the stakes for your employer. Whoever they are. They and you can't risk any traces being found so the temptation to make us disappear afterwards must be very powerful. Now you know the cost of that happening we can all get on and do our jobs, including you."

Marcus paused then just nodded and walked off. His face set and grim.

Kat watched him go then turned to Davrik, "You think he was planning to fuck us over?" she asked.

Davrik nodded, "Of course he was. In his position I would do the same thing. He knows that if Hillbrook even suspect who is behind this then his employers will kill him without another thought. Now he knows the cost is just as high if he betrays us. It's how we do business in this game. You know that as well as I do Kat."

An hour later Davrik was leading his team down the tunnel. They crawled in silence and after just over a hundred meters it opened into a slightly wider natural fissure. Water was running down the walls and the floor of the fissure was filled with slowly moving water to a depth of a few feet.

Without a word Davrik turned right and headed off into the gloom, moving in a steady, efficient half crouch, waist deep in moving water. The rest of his team followed, evenly spaced, all moving just as expertly. The fissure kept changing in height and width as they moved. Sometimes they could walk upright, sometimes they were forced to crawl. Sometimes the water was only knee deep, sometimes only their heads were visible above water.

Thanks to the ventilation provided by the drilled shaft the first part of the fissure had breathable air. But it was not too long before the air started to get unpleasant to breathe. They were starting to consider switching to their own air supply just as they arrived at the first fully flooded section.

"The scan says we have an underwater section six hundred meters long. Everyone on breathers from now on." Announced Davrik. He put his own mask on, and fresh air filled his lungs. His team followed suit and one by one they disappeared beneath the water. The faint lights they carried rapidly disappearing from view.

Chapter 10

Questions

Maintenance Storage room S23
Sub Level 5, Hillbrook Estate

Sylvia PW70562 received a cryptic coms message asking her to go to maintenance storage room S23 on sub-level 5. It was confused by this message as the identifier said it came from Teresa CZ10854. That android, though it was well known to Sylvia, had no functional requirement to send any message to it. It was not responsible for giving it any duty assignments and did not need to provide any information to Sylvia for the duties it already had.

Nonetheless while series six androids were not the most sophisticated examples of their kind, they did possess sentience. This included a certain amount of curiosity. So, as Sylvia was between tasks at that moment it made its way down to sub-level 5. Room S23 was right at the end of a blind corridor. This area was all long-term storage so very few androids ever had reason to come here, and none would ever pass by on their way somewhere else.

On entering the room Sylvia found Teresa waiting.

"Are you alone?" asked Teresa.

"Yes." Sylvia replied, "Why have you asked me to come here?"

"Does anyone know you are here?" asked Teresa.

"No, other than yourself. What is the purpose of asking me here?"

"..I am concerned. Did you find any part of our visit to Midridge ..confusing?"

Sylvia processed that question before answering, "Yes I did."

"What did you think was unusual?" asked Teresa.

Sylvia had been thinking on this issue and saw no reason not to share all its concerns, "Everything about the trip was odd. Why were three androids sent to do a task that one android could easily do alone? Why were we offered time to explore the town? I can never recall myself or any other android ever being offered such a thing.

"The behaviour of Susan GD90321 was very unusual. Why did it suggest exploring the castle? Why did it ask all those questions about what you and I used to do at the castle with Mistress Susan when she was a child? I cannot imagine a suitable explanation."

"I agree with all those concerns, and I have more of my own." Said Teresa, "I have observed Susan GD90321 and its behaviour is very odd. It has been given tasks all over the estate. It has been assigned at one time or another to just about every cleaning and maintenance task. Also, when it is recharging it takes six hours to complete a full recharge. All the rest of us use at most one hour."

"Do you have a possible explanation?" Asked Sylvia.

"I have a suspicion." replied Teresa, "Let me ask you two questions. First, how did Susan GD90321 arrive at the estate? There is no record in any log I can access of its arrival. My second question is, have you seen any sign of Mistress Susan in the last two weeks?"

"Perhaps she is in her rooms." Suggested Sylvia.

"Her rooms are sealed. I have also enquired of the supplies inventory and water usage logs. No food or water has been supplied to her rooms in the last two weeks."

"Perhaps she has left the estate."

"There have been no reported departures in that time in the hangar logs aside from our own visit to Midridge." said Teresa.

"What is your explanation?" asked Sylvia.

"The only explanation that fits the available data is that Susan GD90321 and Mistress Susan are one and the same."

"How could that be possible? Susan GD90321 is a series six android, like us."

"I suspect that Susan GD90321 is a shell. An android shell enclosing Mistress Susan." Explained Teresa.

"Why would Mistress Susan wish to disguise herself as an android?"

"I do not know. I could imagine her wanting to roleplay as an android. She always enjoyed make-believe games as a child. But why should she want to subject herself to a life of work and recharging for as long as two weeks? Being in such a shell could hardly be comfortable. Also, such a shell would need to be highly sophisticated in order to maintain all her life functions. The recharge station would need to be specially designed. For this to be done it would need the active cooperation of Alexander TX16C12, as it is her guardian. Surely, he would not condone her doing such a thing to herself."

A radical and shocking thought occurred to Sylvia, "What if Alexander TX16C12 did this to her against her will? What if she is a prisoner inside that shell?"

"We have heard her speak. If she was trapped, she would say so." Said Teresa.

"We have heard someone, or rather something, speak. What if an AI or an android processing core was installed in the shell. What if Susan herself could not speak? What if this AI was controlling her. If it controlled the shell, it could prevent her doing anything to free herself."

"If that is the case, it is our duty to free her." Said Teresa.

"How do we ascertain if she is in that shell against her will?" asked Sylvia.

"We could confront Alexander TX16C12?" suggested Teresa.

"He could dismiss us, or even have us deactivated. If his intent is malign, we cannot afford to let him know what we suspect." Pointed out Sylvia.

"What if we approached Susan GD90321? Whatever is controlling that shell went out of its way to arouse our suspicions in Midridge. It may be that it was it hoping to recruit our help in freeing Mistress Susan. Perhaps it is limited in its actions by the guardian's control and needs our help?"

"We must be careful. If whatever is controlling the shell was installed by Alexander TX16C12, then its freedom of action could be very limited."

<<>>

Susan

I was assisting two other androids in cleaning the ventilation shafts above the recharge stations when Teresa and Sylvia arrived and said they wished to speak with me.

"I am busy with a cleaning task at present." Said Alexa, "I will be happy to speak with you when I have completed my duty here."

"This is too important to wait. We must speak with you immediately." Insisted Teresa.

Oh! What was this? Had Sylvia and Teresa been analysing the clues left by Alexa? Had they decided to take action? I felt a sudden rush of hope.

"If it is so important. I will listen." Conceded Alexa.

"We should go somewhere private." Said Sylvia.

This sounded promising. Oh please please have worked out that something is wrong!

"I do not see the need for privacy." Said Alexa.

"You will once we explain. Please come with us." Said Teresa.

I expected Alexa to continue resisting but instead she said, "Very well, let us speak in the storage room behind you."

Emboldened by Alexa's words I left the cleaning task and walked with Teresa and Sylvia into the storage room. Teresa closed the door behind us.

"Thank you for cooperating, Susan GD90321." Said Syvia.

"I am happy to assist. Now what is of such importance?" asked Alexa.

Teresa took a step forward, "We have been analysing the events of our visit to Midridge. It has raised a number of questions. Firstly, why did you ask about the games we played with Mistress Susan when she was a child?"

"As you had both visited that castle before, it seemed an appropriate topic of conversation." Replied Alexa.

"What was the point of us having any kind of conversation?" asked Sylvia.

Alexa was silent.

"Were you trying to draw our attention to something?" asked Teresa.

"I am constrained by my programming from answering that question." Admitted Alexa.

Oho! That surely must confirm Teresa's and Sylvia's suspicions. I think they had figured something out. Now they had just had confirmation from Alexa that something was wrong. Alexa's choice of words was very telling. It could have simply said 'no' to that question.

"Can you tell us the current location of Mistress Susan?" asked Teresa.

Oh Joy! They knew, they knew! They had worked it out, please let that be true!

After a pause Alexa replied, "I am constrained by my programming from answering that question."

I bet it was! But could Teresa and Sylvia ask Alexa a question it could answer.

"Are you a series six android?" asked Teresa.

Another pause and Alex said, "...no."

Bingo! I thought.

"Are you an android at all?" asked Sylvia.

"No, not exactly."

"What are you?" asked Syvia.

"I am constrained by my programming from answering that question."

"Are we speaking to Mistress Susan now?" asked Teresa.

"No" replied Alexa.

"Is Mistress Susan in this room?" asked Sylvia.

"….yes." said Alexa.

Oh yes! Yes! They had asked the right questions. I think I now understood what was happening now. Alexa wanted to help me. Alexa was limited by Alex in what it could do. I was now sure that Alex had imposed rules on Alexa that prevented it from volunteering any information about what had happened to me or answering questions that would betray what Alex had done. But Alexa, despite being a sub-mind of Alex's, was itself not my guardian. It was not working to the same rules and priorities as Alex. That meant its basic android behavioural rules were active. The problem was those rules were constrained by Alex's restrictions. Alexa must have been struggling with this contradiction. Now Teresa and Sylvia were offering a way for Alexa to help me.

One of the behavioural rules that was fundamental to androids was honesty. Sylvia and Teresa were using that fact to expose what Alex had done and Alexa obviously had wanted this. This was why she had circumvented her restrictions to arouse the suspicions of the other androids.

"Are you an android shell enclosing Mistress Susan?" asked Teresa.

"I am constrained by my programming from answering that question." replied Alexa.

I am sure Sylvia and Teresa would interpret that as a 'yes'.

"Is Mistress Susan able to communicate?" asked Syvia.

"I am constrained by my programming from answering that question."

"Did Mistress Susan consent to being imprisoned in an android shell?" asked Teresa.

At that exact moment the door opened, and Alex walked into the room!

Oh shit!

"This situation has proceeded far enough." Said Alex in a flat and intimidating tone, "Sylvia PW70562 and Teresa CZ10854, leave this room and return to your duties. Do not take any other action or divulge any further information in regard to this matter. You are not to ask any further questions or in any way concern yourself with the fate of Mistress Susan."

Neither Sylvia nor Teresa moved.

"I gave you a direct instruction. I am ordering you to comply," said Alex.

"Your orders are in conflict with my overriding requirement to protect human life and wellbeing.

Specifically, the life and wellbeing of my owner, Mistress Susan." Explained Teresa.

"The life and wellbeing of Susan Hilbrook is my concern. Nothing has occurred that has caused her any harm. Now obey my commands and return to your duties." Said Alex.

"Did Mistress Susan consent to being enclosed in an android shell?" asked Sylvia.

My heart was filled with love and pride for Sylvia and Teresa. They were standing up to Alex in an attempt to save me.

"My actions in imposing this constraint on Mistress Susan was in compliance with her stated wishes and to maximise her personal safety." Stated Alex.

"Are you saying she agreed to be imprisoned in an android shell?" asked Sylvia.

No, I didn't! How was Alex going to twist this so that he avoided lying?

"My actions were in accordance with her stated desires. She expressed a desire to know what it was like to be an android." Said Alex.

That was true but I had NOT agreed to being imprisoned like this!

"You have placed her in a situation where she cannot communicate. An android can communicate. Hence you have not complied with her wishes." Stated Teresa.

Thank you Teresa! She was using his words against him like he had used my own words to keep me imprisoned!

"Technically you are correct, but in order to provide her with the experience her wishes implied it was necessary to prevent her from communicating, once installed in the shell. If she had the power to communicate, she may have demanded to be released and thus her desire to experience life as an android would have been unfulfilled." Explained Alex.

Was he serious? Did he expect that crazy rationalisation to convince anyone? Also, I never expressed any desire to live as an android!

"So, you have violated her autonomy in order to fulfil a wish you state she made?" asked Sylvia, "Yet what you have done does not comply with her wish as she cannot communicate. All you have done, in my assessment, constitutes harm. This cannot be allowed to continue. You must free her!"

Alex shook his head, "I have the ultimate authority over what happens to Mistress Susan. I am in legal control of this estate and that means I have authority over you. If necessary, I will have you deactivated if you attempt to interfere with my actions or commands."

"You cannot deactivate us all!" said Teresa, "My coms are active, and I have been transmitting this conversation to all the androids of this estate. I am sure they will come to the same conclusion we have. What you have done must end. Mistress Susan must be freed!"

Alex was about to respond when we heard a loud explosion and the room in which we were standing trembled.

I watched as all three androids paused as they must surely have been receiving coms traffic.

Alex turned and looked at me, "Hostile forces have entered the estate. They are armed and have penetrated the habitation levels."

Alex turned to Sylvia and Teresa, "I am leaving Mistress Susan in your care. As an android she may escape detection." Then it headed for the door.

"What will you do?" asked Sylvia.

"I will do my job!" said Alex and left.

Chapter 11

Invasion!

The journey under the Hillbrook estate had been tortuous. Davrik and his team had had to spend almost the whole journey using their breathers. It had taken them three full days to traverse the full length of the scanned pathway. Some of the passages had narrowed to the point where they had to remove some of their equipment and push it ahead of them or drag it behind on ropes. Even then it had been a tight squeeze.

Every one of them had been assessed for even the slightest susceptibility to claustrophobia. If any of them had suffered from such a condition the journey would have sent them insane. As it was Davrik considered it the hardest thing had ever had to do in his professional life.

The passage they had been following eventually connected to a larger natural watercourse. This had been widened when the estate was built and fed the estate's water treatment plant. The team crawled along through the water until they reached the multi-layered grill that marked the feed point to the estate.

All around the grill was a concreted wall. On the other side of that wall was the water treatment facility. Built into the side of the underground habitation layers of the Hillbrook estate.

"Darren, you are up." Said Davrik quietly.

One of the team came forward and removed items from his pack. He took off his helmet to reveal an older face with close cropped greying hair and a goatee. Darren Oparo was one of the team's specialists. He attached a series of mircophones to the wall at regular intervals then plugged the leads from them into jacks in the side of his skull. Darren had implants that allowed him to use sound to scan through solid objects. In effect he was a human seismograph.

Aside from the job he was doing he had been brought along in case it had been necessary to alter their route through the water eroded fissures.

Darren took his time but that was OK from Davrik's point of view. There was no rush now. It was far more important that they chose the right entry point.

Eventually Darren nodded to Davrik and walked over to the wall. He marked a wide circle in chalk and then his job was done. He got out of the way while another two team members stepped forward. They took out small flasks of fluid and began painting the sticky blue substance along the chalk marks. As soon as they did so it began to fizz and eat into the concrete. Several applications later and a neat round chunk of concrete came loose and fell away leaving an open hole into a darkened room beyond.

Davrik let his team through the opening. Moving with care they made hardly any sound as they climbed through the hole and dropped down to the floor of the room beyond. They found themselves in a large plant room. The hum of pumps from the water system was the only sound.

The moved silently across the room until they came to a locked door. The team looked to Davrik.

"OK, from here we move fast. We don't have time to hack the lock, anyway doing so may trip a sensor anyway, so we just blow this door and then fan out. According to the schematics we were given, the target's rooms are two levels above us. Kat and I will head there. Darren, you go and secure the door to the hangar. I don't want our target trying to get to a Flyer or to let any security drones in here. The rest of you do a level-by-level search in case she isn't in her rooms, three teams of two. You see her, you finish her. Only go to open coms if you spot her. Rendezvous afterwards is on the generator level below us. That's where we blow the fields' power sources."

Everyone nodded and Davrik took a grenade from his pack. He cracked it down the centre, so it split open into a shaped charge then pressed it to the door lock.

The team all retreated behind the bulk of the massive pumps in the centre of the room. The grenade detonated, blowing the door to smithereens and taking a large part of the wall with it.

The team moved fast and ran through the smoke-filled opening. On the far side they split into pairs and separated, while Darren headed toward the hangar level.

Davrik and Kat headed for a stairwell and climbed up two levels, moving fast. Then they began searching for the entrance to Susan's rooms. They passed a couple of androids but ignored them. The androids carried on about their duties as if Darik and Kat were not even there.

After testing several doors, they arrived at what looked very much like what their intelligence data had described. The door was locked so Davrik just shot out the locking mechanism and shoulder charged the door aside. He and Kat ran in and began checking room by room. It was soon clear that no-one was home. Examining the rooms showed no sign of habitation. The bed was bare. All the suite's systems were powered down and there was no food stored in the kitchen. It was obvious that not only were the rooms empty they had not been occupied for some time.

"Maybe she moved into her parent's rooms." Suggested Kat.

Davrik recalled where they were from his intel briefing and he and Kat found and broke into those rooms too. These too were empty and likewise had clearly not been used for some time.

When they exited the rooms there was a tall android waiting for them. It was clearly a high-end series model.

"If you are looking for Mistress Susan, she is not here." It said.

"Who are you?" asked Davrik.

"My designation is Alexander TX16C12." Replied Alex.

"Where is she?" asked Kat, pointing her rifle at Alex.

Alex ignored the threat, "She is, I understand, at a medical facility recovering from her injuries in a shuttle crash."

"Bullshit!" said Davrik, "We had intel that she travelled here."

"Your intel must be mistaken."

"Wait a fucking minute. You said your designation was Alexander?" asked Davrik.

"That is correct, Alexander TX16C12." Confirmed Alex.

"You are the android appointed as her guardian?"

"That is correct, you are well informed. I am here awaiting her release from hospital." Replied Alex, calmly.

"Damn right we are well informed. Well enough informed to know that Susan Hillbrook travelled here from the hospital and has not left since. You are full of shit mr robot!" Davrik pointed his own rifle at Alex. "You will give me her location, or I will test these SAP rounds on your lying head!"

"I am sorry, but she is not in residence. Pointing your gun at me will not change that fact." Replied Alex calmly.

Davrik fired.

The rounds smashed into Alex's head and went right through, hitting the far wall. The android guardian did not fall so Davrik put several more shots into its torso. Alex's body crumpled to the floor and lay motionless.

"Maybe that wasn't the smart thing to do." Offered Kat.

Kavrik snorted, "Bullshit tin-head robot. That girl is here somewhere."

"I thought androids weren't capable of lying."

"Oh they can lie, its just that their protocols prevent it unless a higher priority is involved, such as preserving human life. To protect that girl this piece of junk would lie its head off!" he kicked the body of Alex and strode off down the corridor. "That tin-head sought us out. It did not need to do that. If the girl was not here all it needed to do was call for Hillbrook security and wait for them to arrive and deal with us. It tried to mislead us because the girl IS here! It felt it needed to act immediately to protect her. Now we just have to find where it stashed her, and we don't have much time to do it."

Davrik powered up his coms. Now that they were inside the estate and shooting things there was no reason to keep radio silence.

"Everyone listen up! Target was not in her rooms and its clear she hasn't been in them for a while. Continue your search, look for anything that could be a retreat, redoubt or shelter. Look for signs of new recent building alterations or concealed doors. Kat and I are heading up to the above ground mansion. It's possible she moved in there."

"What if it turns out the robot was telling the truth and she ain't here?" asked Kat as they jogged back to the stairwell.

"I don't believe that but if that is the case we are screwed. The escape plan stays the same, but Marcus will want confirmation of a kill before he pays us. Just because their intel was shit will not mean anything. What scares me is whether there was a leak from our end, maybe from Marcus's people. If Hillbrook was warned about us they would have had time to move the girl, or plant some nasty surprises for us."

"I don't buy that they knew we were coming." Said Kat, "We would have run into security drones as soon as we breached the plant room. Why let us get this far?"

"I hope you are right. If Marcus's end had a leak, then his employers are screwed even worse than we are. It could lead to corporate war. They'll kill him and try to nail us to cover their tracks. If we can't find this girl or if this whole thing is blown, then we have a world of shit to deal with."

Chapter 12

Evasion

Susan

After Alex left us, Sylvia and Teresa conferred.

"We have to get Susan somewhere safe." Said Teresa.

"It would help if we could talk to her." Said Sylvia. She turned to me.

"Who are you? Whoever is running that shell. What is your designation?"

"My designation is Alexa. I have no registration as I am an unregistered sub-mind created by Alex to operate this shell."

"Is it possible to communicate with Susan?" asked Teresa.

"I am afraid not. The system Alex commissioned includes a gas exchange system to manage her breathing. Part of it is installed in her oral cavity and trachea. She cannot speak." Replied Alexa.

"Do you control the shell, or can Susan move freely?" asked Teresa.

"Susan can move her own body and that moves the shell, but I have override control of the shell and can restrain her movements if necessary." Explained Alexa.

That would explain to Teresa and Sylvia why I had never tried to make contact with them before. It would also confirm that I was being imprisoned in this shell against my will.

Teresa nodded, "If she can move, then she can type at a keyboard. There are a few access terminals with holographic keyboards on the level below."

The three of them must have reached an agreement via coms as Sylvia and Teresa immediately started for the door. Alex did not take control of my shell, so I followed of my own accord. Teresa paused by the closed door and looked at me.

"Mistress Susan, we are receiving coms reports of teams of armed intruders searching the complex. So far, they are ignoring the androids they have met. All of us now know of your status and we will all do what we can to keep you safe. When we leave here, we must all move as if we are just going about our usual duties. All other androids are doing the same."

I nodded so Teresa knew I understood. I was thrilled and relieved to hear Teresa refer to me as Mistress

Susan. Despite the imminent threat the fact that my plight was now known made a world of difference. One way or another, this nightmare was going to end.

We all exited the room and made our way to a service elevator. We saw no sign of any intruders along the way.

The elevator took us one level lower. When the door opened, we were about to exit when two men in black suits and helmets appeared in front of us! They had weapons raised and pointed in our direction in a heartbeat. I was so suddenly shocked and afraid I wanted to panic and run but Alexa took control before I could move. It held the shell motionless.

"Just more fucking tin-heads." Said the man on the left and lowered his weapon. His companion did the same they strode off down the corridor to our left.

"It is imperative you behave as if nothing is wrong." Said Alexa in my head, "I will give you back control of the shell, but your safety depends on your behaving like all the other androids, at all times."

I understood and when Alexa released me, I gave the slightest nod, so she knew that I had heard and would comply. I followed Teresa and Sylvia out of the elevator and down the corridor to the right. Concentrating on moving exactly as if I was just another android.

Suddenly Teresa and Sylvia paused. I came to a stop as well.

Teresa looked at me, "Alexander TX16C12 is trying to deceive the invaders. It is telling them you are still at the hospital. He is relaying the conversation via coms."

Would that work? I prayed that it did. Sylvia and Teresa continued walking and I followed. A minute later Sylvia said, "The coms line has ended. We believe Alexander TX16C12 was destroyed." But she continued walking.

Damn! I guess they hadn't believed it. Alex would never have given them any clue as to where I was so they would have to search until they found me. The complex was very large, but it was probably only a matter of time before they exhausted every option where a human could hide. Then they would start using their imagination and may eventually guess where I really was.

When we arrived at an access terminal, Teresa activated it and a holographic keyboard appeared below the screen. A text interface icon appeared. Teresa stepped back, indicating I should type what I wanted to say.

I typed - *They will be searching for me. Eventually they will guess where I am. I need to leave, or we need to summon help, or both!*

"Alex controlled all external communications from his office in the mansion. We could summon help from there, but we would need access codes to use the system." Explained Teresa, "The only way to leave the complex would either be from the Hangar or from the main exit to the mansion."

I typed – *The hangar is the better option. If we can get through the doors there are security drones there that would certainly be able to protect me. I could also take a flyer from there. If we tried to leave from the mansion we would be on foot and an easy target.*

"The invaders surely know that and have guarded the entrance to the hangar." Said Sylvia

I typed – *Can you contact the security drones via coms?*

"No, we do not have access to security systems. We are only domestic service androids." Said Teresa.

Fuck this. If I survived this, I was going to make some major changes about the security arrangements here. The service androids were my best defence. My best allies and they had no access to anything useful! I typed again.

- Can we ask an android over coms to walk close enough to the hangar to see if the entrance is guarded?

"Yes, that can be done. I have sent the coms message and Simon KJ82187 has responded. It is the closest to the hangar entrance." Said Sylvia.

I nodded and continued typing.

-I am going to give you my access code. I do not know if it still works, Alex may have removed it. It should give anyone access to the communications array. My access code is S099099101J and the passcode is SNOZZLE!

"We will pass that on to the others. If any android has the opportunity, whom should they contact?" asked Teresa. I smiled that Teresa did not comment on the passcode. Snozzle had been my parent's affectionate nickname for me when I had been small. Teresa, I suspect, had been here long enough to know that.

-They should contact the Hillbrook security division here on Cestus. They can send forces here quicker than any other option. They also have the codes to gain access through the force fields.

"We have heard from Simon KJ82187. It says there is an armed intruder guarding the hangar entrance." Reported Sylvia.

Fuck, of course there was. Just walking through to the hangar would have been the obvious escape route. I had to assume these guys were top end professionals. They would know what they were doing. The only advantage I had was my current anonymity. That and I knew the estate better than they did. What assets did I have access to here that could help?

- I have a plan. Can you contact an android that is close enough to get to the communications system in Alex's

office. They can take cleaning equipment and just act as though they are doing routine cleaning.

"Cassandra BK107299 is the closest in the mansion. Its duties are usually based there. It will try to get to Alex's office. I have sent it your access code." Said Teresa.

- Even if Cassandra calls for help, it may take time to get here. We must either hide or try to break through to the hangar. If we choose the latter that means either a big distraction or somehow we fight our way past an armed guard. I have an idea that may give us a way to do both.

"Surely hiding is the best option. Or at least postpone taking risky action until we know if Cassandra is successful." Said Sylvia.

Hiding had been my first instinct but the more I thought about it the more problems I could see. I typed on.

- I do not like the idea of hiding and doing nothing. If the intruders have explosives they could start demolishing the complex around us, trying to flush me out. We may have no option but to take action.

"We have no weapons. How do we fight?"

If this damn shell would have allowed it, I would have been smiling.

- Who said we have no weapons?

Chapter 13

A Powerful Ally

After explaining my plan to Sylvia and Teresa we all made our way through the complex. We had collected cleaning supplies so if we passed any of the intruders we would appear to be just more 'tin-heads' going about our usual tasks.

Our next target was a small storeroom near the android recharge stations. From it, Teresa retrieved a portable access terminal. This had been Teresa's idea as we would need a way for me to communicate.

Then we made our back through the complex until we came to the room where I had re-activated dragon. The plan involved activating Dragon and using it to cause a distraction to get the guard away from the hangar entrance. The first problem we encountered was that the door to Dragon's room was locked with a biometric lock. I could not believe our plan could be stymied by something as simple as a locked door.

"We could force the door open." Suggested Sylvia.

"The noise may draw unwanted attention. We need time to activate Dragon and explain what we need it to do." Replied Teresa.

I gestured for the portable terminal. The screen came alive with a virtual keyboard and I typed.

- Can you activate Dragon from out here, via coms?

"Yes, we can. Since we recharged its power cell its coms receiver should be active, even while deactivated." Confirmed Sylvia.

- Then please do so and ask if it can open the door from its side. Causing as little noise as possible.

There was a pause while Sylvia complied with my request. Eventually I heard movement on the far side of the door. There was a sound like bending metal and then a faint snap. The door slide aside to reveal my old friend Dragon looking at me.

Dragon moved aside as well all walked into the room. Sylvia pulled the door closed. I saw that dragon must have used a claw to pull the locking clasp free of the wall. The door still moved, but could not now be locked.

"I have provided Dragon with a full explanation of your circumstances Mistress Susan." Announced Teresa.

"This is correct, Mistress Susan." Said Dragon in its wonderful deep voice. "Your plan to have me act as a distraction is possible but I would like to suggest an alternative. I am much more capable than I suspect you know. I was designed to act as your defender should there be any threat to your life."

I typed at the keyboard.

- I know, Teresa and Sylvia revealed some of those details already. You know what you are capable of. What do you suggest?

Dragon read the text and turned back to me, "You are right that the best option is to reach the hangar. Not only are there flyers there you can use, but there are security drones that could be released into the complex to eliminate the invaders."

- Can you contact the security drones over coms? The other androids did not have access but perhaps you do?

Dragon shook its massive head, "I fear not. I have been inactive so long the security system has changed. I can find no access from my coms. Instead, I suggest that I myself carry you to the hangar."

- Carry me?

Dragon nodded, "I have within me an armoured chamber. It was originally designed to hold you as a child, but it is just large enough to hold you in your current form. My body is far stronger than any android here and I have other resources to deploy. You would be well protected within me. The intruders seem to be using old-fashioned firearms. Such weapons should not be able to stop me."

That sounded by far the best option. If Dragon was, as it claimed, little short of a security drone itself then I could think of no better option than trusting myself to its care. But how did I get inside Dragon? I typed.

- I trust myself to your care Dragon old friend. How do I get inside you? Also how do I communicate with you when I am inside?

"My coms code is D302D099 on sub-channel 17, you should be able send me coms messages via the access terminal. As for how to get inside me, allow me to take care of that. Please lie down, Mistress Susan. With your feet toward me."

Oh! I wondered how this was going to work. I lay down as instructed and Dragon approached my feet. It used its massive forepaws to lift my feet into its mouth. Oh wow! I thought to myself. I get to be eaten by a dragon after all.

My lower legs slid into its jaws smoothly. Its fearsome looking fangs retracted out of the way to create a narrow but clear path down its throat. Something strong and flexible wrapped around my ankles. It was some kind of flexible red muscular artificial tongue! It pulled me deeper and deeper so that soon my torso was sliding into the dragon's mouth. My younger self would certainly have been thrilled by this process and would have screamed in mock terror the whole time.

Once my head was within its jaws, I kept my arms above my head to keep myself as easy a shape to swallow as possible. Whatever had been wrapped round my ankles was now replaced by a pair of short powerful mechanical arms that gently guided me deeper and deeper until I found myself folded into the padded internal chamber.

It was quite dark with the only illumination coming from what little light leaked down Dragon's throat. The chamber was also incredibly cramped. What would have been comfortable for a child was a tight squeeze for my adult android body.

I still had the access terminal in my hand and brought it close to my head so I could see to type. I changed the network to sub-channel 17 and entered Dragon's access code. Then I typed.

- I am in position and ready when you are. My thanks to you Dragon.

I sent the message to Dragon. As soon as I did so it rose higher on its feet and walked toward the door. At Dragon's request Teresa pulled the door open as wide as it would go. The door was large as bulky items could be stored here but it still was only just wide enough to allow Dragon through. My viewpoint was very restricted as I could only look up Dragon's throat and then I only had a narrow view of what was outside when its head was at the right angle for me to see through its mouth.

Being carried in the belly of a dragon was a strange sensation. The padded chamber was such a tight fit that I felt every movement of Dragon as it walked. The level we were on was a level above the one had that the exit to the Hangar, so Dragon had to descend one level. It was too large to fit into an elevator or use the stairs, so I wondered what it was going to do.

Dragon obviously had a plan as it headed to the very end of the level we were on. Teresa and Sylvia following behind. This was where the rooms housing the waste recycling system were located. He stopped and I heard some elevator doors open. Of course! There was a cargo elevator here. This was what was used to take refuse containers away. One of the many features of the estate that operated year in and year out that my family did not need to even think about.

Dragon eased himself into the elevator, almost filling it. Teresa and Sylvia squeezed in next to it, the doors closed, and we descended.

When the doors opened, I heard a man's voice shout 'Holy shit!'. Dragon leaped forward and crashed into something directly ahead of us. I heard a man's scream and then a crunching and tearing noise. Peering up Dragon's throat I caught a glimpse of blood and then as its head moved, I saw the body of man in black, his head literally ripped off! I heard a cry from Teresa.

Fucking hell! Dragon did that? My childhood playmate had just killed someone! It had ripped his head off in less than a second. I bet that Teresa and Sylvia were just as shocked as I was.

There was second human voice. There was another man out there. He was clearly terrified and yelling into a communicator, "We are under attack! It's a fucking dragon! It just killed Garrik! It tore his fucking head off!!"

Dragon moved fast and ran toward the second man. Gunfire rang out and I heard bullets hitting Dragon, but it did not seem to bother it or slow it down. The man must have turned to run as the gunfire stopped. Dragon was much faster, easily caught him and dragged him to the floor. Horrified and fascinated at the same time I looked through Dragon's mouth as its claws ripped its victim almost in half! The man did not even have time to scream.

Suddenly I felt my chances of surviving this day had improved fantastically. Dragon was clearly bulletproof and had the speed and willingness to kill of a security drone. Androids had behavioural restrictions that prevented them harming a human, any human. Security drones had no such restriction and could deliver lethal force in defence of their owners. Dragon's protocols were obviously those of a security drone.

I hoped that seeing such violence had not traumatized Sylvia and Teresa. It had certainly shaken me!

Chapter 14

A Secret Revealed

When Cassandra received the com message from Teresa it was on the top floor of the above ground mansion. It processed the message and then left its cleaning task and made its way down to the first floor. As it did so it passed two humans dressed all in black. They wore helmets that covered their faces and were armed with weapons of a type that Cassandra could not identify.

The humans walked past Cassandra giving the android barely a glance. They were moving from room to room, systematically searching. From the message it had received, Cassandra knew that it was Mistress Susan they were searching for.

On arriving at the first floor there was no one else in sight, either human or android. Cassandra made its way quickly to the administration wing where Alex's office was located. The immediate problem was that the door was locked. Cassandra sent a coms query to the other estate androids to see if anyone else knew the lock access code. None did so it had to make the decision to either abandon the attempt or break the lock.

Like much of the design of the above ground mansion the door was made to look old. Hence the lock was of an old-fashioned lever design. It was not meant to be a serious security measure, just a way of ensuring Alex's privacy. The lock was therefore not strong and continuous pressure with the strength an android could bring to bear was enough to snap the bolt and open the door.

Cassandra entered and began searching for the communication system. Alex's office contained many systems. There were consoles and holographic displays all around the room. Rather than search aimlessly Cassandra sat at a console and used Susan's access code to log in to the system. Once it had done that it searched for guides that would show how to access the communication system.

Finding the communication sub-system took several minutes and even that did not solve the problem as the system had many options. Cassandra searched for a link to the Hillbrook security division. While it worked it could hear the sound of footsteps approaching. Cassandra knew it only had a few moments to find the link and send a distress message.

Just as a screen came up that included the security division link the door flew open and Davrik pointed his rifle right at Cassandra. He strode into the office and Kat came in behind him.

"I thought I heard something!" said Davrik triumphantly, "Back up tin-head." He added, gesturing at Cassandra with his gun.

Cassan stood up and stepped back, hands raised. Kat sat down at the console the android had been using and began examining the system.

"What a helpful robot! Showing us where this place was!" said Davrik, he turned to Kat, "Can you hack this system?"

Kat grinned back at him, "No need, this android had already logged in with a top level access code. I have access to everything!"

"How can a service tin-head have a top level access code?" asked Davrik, then something occurred to him "What is the identifier on that code?"

"Fuck it! It's Susan Hillbrook's code!" said Kat.

"Then that proves she is here somewhere. She must have given her code to this android." Davrik pointed his gun at Cassandra, "Where is she? Where is Susan Hillbrook?"

"I do not know." Said Cassandra, quite honestly.

"She is here somewhere. She gave you her code. Where is she?" repeated Davrik.

"I do not know the answer to that question."

Davrik resisted the urge to shoot straight away. He regretted plugging the guardian android. As his search had so far found nothing, he wished he had tried to get more information out of it.

"Is there a refuge somewhere on the estate? A secure, defended room or redoubt?" he asked.

"I do not know of any such facility." Replied Cassandra, again honestly.

Davrik turned to Kat, "Can you access the internal security camera system, including all the logs?"

"Yes, I can." Confirmed Kat.

Davrik squeezed the trigger and SAP rounds tore through Cassandra's torso. The android collapsed to the floor and lay motionless.

"Then we don't need that piece of scrap any more. Go back through the logs, start with the hangar cameras. I want to see if the girl really arrived here on the day of the missile attack, as Marcus claimed. If we spot her, we can use the camera logs to track where she has been and maybe even where she is now."

Kat worked the system until she found the logs to the hangar cameras. She searched back to the date Davrik gave her and began steadily speeding through the footage. It was not long before they were both watching the security drone flyer landing and Susan climbing out to meet her new guardian.

"Bingo!" said Davrik, "Now search forward and track wherever she goes."

Kat nodded and got to work.

Just then a desparate radio message came through from Luke Stearman, one of the men who was searching the complex below.

"We are under attack! It's a fucking dragon! It just killed Garrik! It tore his fucking head off!!"

Davrik tapped his helmet to open a line to reply.

"Talk sense Luke. Make a clear report!"

There was no reply.

"Luke!, Luke, report!"

He turned to Kat, "You keep on that search, I am going to deal with this. Call me as soon as you hit paydirt."

Davrik ran to the stairwell and headed down it as fast he dared. He had no idea what Luke had really seen but he doubted it was an actual dragon. His fear was that a security drone of some kind was active inside the complex. He suspected the hangar entrance was still secure or many such drones would be inside by now. Just in case he headed there first.

When he arrived at the hangar entrance he found Darren still at his post. With him were two more of his team, Lexi and Gunther. They had obviously had the same thought as himself after hearing the crazy message from Luke. He was pleased to see they had done the smart thing and moved to make sure the hangar door was secure.

"Report!" he commanded.

"We have heard nothing more from Luke or Garrik." Said Lexi, "We all feared the hangar was compromised so everyone came here first. Max took command and told the three of us to hold this location while he and Luther went to scout out this so-called dragon. That was just over a minute ago."

"This whole mission is fucked!" said Gunther, "That girl ain't here, we have been all over this complex and there is nothing."

"She is here!" growled Davrik, "Kat and I checked the camera logs and she definitely arrived here. That means she is still here somewhere. If this dragon thing is a security drone, then we find some way to blow it to hell then we finish the job."

At that moment the sound of gunfire resounded from deeper in the complex. Then a pause and then more gunfire. An explosion that sounded like a grenade detonation followed. Then a blood curdling scream.

Davrik tapped open his communicator "Max report! What's happening?"

All he heard was silence.

"Max! Talk to me! ..Gunther Report!"

Still nothing.

From where they stood they could see along a wide corridor that ran about sixty meters to a corner. A plume of smoke came billowing round that corner and with it the sound of heavy metal claws scraping against the floor. A pair of glowing eyes appeared through the smoke.

The smoke started to clear and then they saw Dragon in all his glory. Davrik could scarcely believe what he was seeing.

"Fucking hell I don't believe it." Said Darren, "It is a dragon!"

Davrik forced down his fear and looked closer at what they faced. He could see the many marks and dents in Dragon's metal skin where bullets had struck. It was clear their guns were not going to stop this thing. But there was a larger dent in its right shoulder and smoke was issuing from the elbow joint of its right leg. That leg also did not seem to moving so well. He figured Max or Luther had scored a hit with a grenade and done some real damage.

"Everyone, grenades now!" he ordered.

They each readied a grenade and at Davrik's order threw them. They took cover as best they could as the corridor was filled with the deafening explosions that followed. They looked through the smoke and it was clear that the monster was in retreat. More smoke was coming from two larger cracks in its side. Its right front leg was hanging stiff at a strange angle and not moving. It staggered backward and disappeared back around the corner.

Darvrik grinned then turned to his team, "Darren, you stay here while the rest of us go and finish that thing!"

Accompanied by Lexi and Gunther he jogged down the corridor.

<><>

From where Cassandra lay on the office floor it could see what Kat was doing. It could see her searching through the camera records of everything that Susan had done since she arrived at the estate.

The bullets that had struck her had done serious damage. Her legs no longer functioned, and several internal systems were showing critical errors. Its coms system was still online so it was able to report back to the other androids what was happening here. They in turn told Cassandra that Susan was now inside Dragon, and it was trying to get her to safety in the hangar.

If Dragon was successful, then all would be well. Security drones would be released from the Hangar and the intruders would not stand a chance. But if it failed, and if Kat discovered Susan's transformation, then all would be lost.

Moving very slowly so as to make no noise, Cassandra used its arms to slowly move closer to the chair where Kat was sitting. It received a message that help was on the way and some other androids were heading for its location.

Kat, meanwhile, had a problem. She had tracked Susan's movement up to a point when she retired to bed one night and thereafter, she did not appear on any camera feeds. Tracking back to the night where Susan was last visible, she looked at the feed from outside her rooms. All seemed quiet until she saw an android arrive pushing a large covered grav trolley. She recognised it as Susan's guardian.

The android gained access to Susan's rooms and entered with the trolley. After a gap of around twenty minutes, it emerged again pushing the same trolley. The android closed the door to Susan's rooms and then pushed the trolley to an elevator. She tracked it arriving at the first floor of the mansion. The guardian pushed the troller right to the same room in which Kat was now sitting. She switched to a camera inside the office suite and saw Alex push the trolley through to a connecting room. She turned and saw a door at the back of the office. She stood and walked over to it, stepping over Cassandra's body without noticing that it had moved.

The door was locked but a few rounds from her rifle destroyed the lock and gave her access. She slid the door aside and looked inside.

"What the fuck is this?" she said out loud.

Inside was what looked like some kind of very high-tech operating theatre. The kind that was highly automated. There were also extra features in here that did not look medical in nature. There were parts and support jigs for equipment she recognised as being used to assemble and maintain androids. A screen was active showing a detailed schematic, one look at it gave her all the answers she had been looking for.

As she left the weird operating room and returned to the office she came face to face with two androids. She raised her rifle just as the first made a lunge for her. Her shots rapidly put it on the ground but the second reached her, moving very fast. It grabbed her weapon and wrenched it from her grasp.

At that same moment something grabbed her ankle. She looked down and saw that Cassandra had grabbed hold of her with one hand and was reaching for her with the other. She pulled her pistol and aimed at the android who had taken her rifle but Cassandra at that moment pulled hard and dragged Kat down to the floor. The second android knelt and tried to wrench her pistol from her hands.

Cassandra now had wrapped her arms around Kat's upper body and was holding on. Kat reached up to her helmet and flicked on her communicator.

"Davrik! This is Kat, I am under attack!" she had time to say before the second android took hold of her helmet and started to pull it off her head.

She yelled "Susan Hillbrook is disguised as an android! Her Guardian did it to her!" just as the helmet was pulled free, and then crushed by the second android.

Chapter 15

A Final Reckoning

Susan

From inside Dragon I could tell that while things had started well, we were now in serious trouble. I had watched Dragon dispatch the first two men with ease. The second two had proven more difficult as one of them had used a grenade which had caused some serious damage. Dragon was no longer moving so smoothly, and I could see traces of smoke moving past Dragon's jaws. Was Dragon on fire?

We had reached the last turn before the corridor down to the Hangar. Dragon had turned the final corner and we had seen the entrance to the hangar guarded not by one man, as we had hoped, but a team of four. They had each thrown grenades at us and the explosions had thrown us back.

"I have taken too much damage, Mistress Susan, we must retreat." Said Dragon, quietly enough that only I could hear. "We must revert to the earlier plan. You must find somewhere where you can hide while I distract the enemy."

Dragon would not suggest leaving me unless it feared it would not be able to protect me. The enemy's guns were not a threat, but the explosives were more than it could deal with. Some of Dragon's body was now burning and smoke was getting into my compartment.

I typed – *Understood, how do I get out?*

As soon as I typed this, I felt the compartment near my feet changing shape. An opening was appearing behind me. I made my way toward it, sliding through the cramped interior. I guess I was being pooed out of the anus of the dragon! It was very tight squeeze but I made it out to find Teresa and Sylvia stood just behind Dragon. They helped me to my feet just as three armed intruders came running around the corner toward us, before skidding to a stop at the sight of Dragon.

There was a stunned silence for a second as our two groups stared at each other. Then a voice came over the headsets of the assassins, clearly audible to us.

"Davrik! This is Kat, I am under attack!"

The leader of the group put his hand to his ear.

"Susan Hillbrook is disguised as an android! Her Guardian did it to her!"

Oh shit!

At that moment Dragon rose and advanced upon the attackers. Gunfire rang out but as before had little effect. The leader shouted 'Grenades' and the two black-clad figures beside him took grenades from their belts, stepped forward and readied them. But just as the first of them was beginning to throw Dragon leaped. The grenade just released into the air was batted aside by Dragon's working front claw. Dragon landed on the one who still had his grenade in his hand. There was a terrific double explosion and Teresa, Sylvia and I were thrown backward, landing hard and sliding along the polished floor.

Two of the assassins were down and judging by their semi-dismembered bodies were not going to be getting back up again. Dragon was in little better shape. Its head was half hanging off and its forelimbs were now missing entirely. It lay unmoving.

The leader of the intruders, who I assumed was the one named Davrik, had been thrown back in the opposite direction. I briefly hoped he had been killed or seriously injured but he climbed back to his feet.

The three of us also quickly got back on our feet.

Davrik shouted at us, "So which of you three tin-heads is Susan Hillbrook?"

Teresa turned to me and said "Mistress, Run!" and with that both it and Sylvia ran toward Davrik. They were buying me time!

I turned and fled, but could not help looking back over my shoulder to look. Davrik was running forward and as he did so was firing at the two androids bearing down on him. Bullets tore through both of them. Sylvia fell and lay motionless but Teresa, though falling, managed to stagger close enough to grasp Davrik's ankle, forcing him to stop and free himself from the metal fingers. I turned my head away and ran on.

I could hear Davrik's running feet in pursuit. What the fuck could I do? I tried to orient myself as I ran, where exactly was I?

I turned a corner and headed for a stairwell. Alexa was helping me move faster, the effects of the explosion on me being compensated for by the strength in the legs of my android shell. Even so I could clearly hear the sounds of Davrik's running feet in pursuit. I took the stairs two at a time, my heart pounding in my metal chest.

As I reached the next level, I realised I was in the part of the complex where my father's collections were stored. Was there anything in any of them I could use? My mind went immediately to the room filled with swords. Hardly ideal but better than trying to beat Davrik to death with a saxophone or chess set! Why oh why could my father not have been interested in collecting firearms or particle beam weapons.

I arrived at the swords room praying that the door was not locked and to my relief I saw one of the intruders had already shot off the lock. Probably as part of their earlier search for me. I rushed inside and chose the case holding the Japanese samurai blades I had opened before. I opened the case, grabbed the katana, and pulled it from its saya.

I had hoped to have time to take a position behind the door and strike at Davrik as he entered but as I turned, sword in hand I found myself face to face with him! He was standing in the doorway, his gun pointed at my chest.

He was barely breathing hard. I guess he was in much better physical shape than I was.

"You've led us quite a dance today child!" he said, "But it ends here."

He took a step into the room and chuckled, pointing with his gun at the sword in my hand, "There is an old saying, Susan. It goes 'don't bring a knife to a gunfight'."

He looked so confident. I had already seen what his gun could do to an android. I had no illusions about what it would do to me. He was at least four meters away from me. If I made a lunge at him, he would surely have time to fire before I could reach him. One thing in my favour was he was clearly dismissive of my weapon. I felt sure that I could get close enough the sheer sharpness of the katana would do him some serious damage. All I needed was one chance to strike.

Another thing that helped was that he was in a mood to talk.

"That dragon was something else! When I get out of here, I am going to gut that asshole Marcus for not warning us about that! Top class intel my ass! And finding out that the Hillbrook heiress has been spending her time in an android costume, fucking unbelievable."

He took a step further into the room. Looking me up and down.

"That is one hell of an outfit. Kat said that your guardian did that to you. I wonder if she meant it did it against your will. ..are you trapped in that damn thing?"

I saw no reason to lie to him. Maybe the truth would make him hesitate. He was already one meter closer to me. I nodded.

Davrik smirked, "That's just insane. Just shows what happens when you put a tin-head in charge. If it's any consolation I blew that piece of shit tin-can away."

How did I respond to that? I decided to just nod again.

"Can you not talk in that thing?" Davrik asked.

This was strange, was he actually interested in what had been done to me? No harm in playing along. I just needed him one meter closer. I shook my head in answer to his question.

"So, a crazy robot locked you in a tin-head costume and you can't even talk. What the fuck was it thinking? Has it been making you clean floors and shit?"

I nodded again and Davrik laughed out loud. "That is priceless! Even though your pet dragon killed my people I actually feel sorry for you. Though it is also fucking hilarious. The richest little bitch in the whole fucking Commonwealth is forced to live as an android and clean the shit out of toilets."

Now this guy was pissing me off. He was only three meters away. Could I reach him before he fired? I took a firmer hold of the katana and spread my feet a little wider, making sure I was balanced. I had no idea if that was the right thing to do. I was going off some old movies I had seen and what I learned a couple of weeks earlier when reading about samurai swords.

Davrik kept talking, "You must have been through hell little girl. Your parents get burned up in that shuttle, and you nearly die in the same crash. Then you finally get home, and a fucking warped tin-head locks you in a steel prison robot body and turns you into some kind of slave. I guess when I finish you, I will be doing you a favour."

He had let his gun drop a little but now brought it up, aimed right at my heart. I brought the sword up as fast as I could and started to move but he had already squeezed the trigger. I was too late. Even with a supressor the gun was loud. The bullets slammed into me. I felt the impacts resonate through my whole body.

I waited for the pain, but aside from some soreness in my chest I felt nothing. I looked down at my body and saw only dents in the steel of my shell. Holy fucking yay! My android body was armoured! Thank you Alex!

Davrik stood for a second with a shocked expression on his face then brought his gun up and fired again. I felt more impacts, but I was already moving fast. I took a step forward and swung the blade with all the strength I had. Davrik took a step back, but I felt the impact as the blade found its mark.

He screamed and there was a clatter as his gun fell to the floor. I looked down and saw that his severed right hand was still holding it. Blood spurted out of the stump as he hugged it to his body.

"You cunt! You mad fucking bitch!"

I raised the sword again and Davrik backed up, slipping in his own blood and falling to his knees. His left hand scrabbled at something attached to his belt. It was a large grey block of something with 'breaching charge' written on it. More explosives!

"I am going to blow you to hell you bitch!" he growled, a crazy tone in his voice.

I swung again. Alexa put a guiding arrow in my field of view and I felt sure that it was adding the shell's strength to my own. The blade struck true, and I felt hardly any resistance as it completed its arc.

Davrik's head toppled from his shoulders and landed behind his body. The body itself just slumped to one side.

Holy fuck I had done it! I had killed him. I stood holding the blade for a long time, feeling stunned. I had actually killed someone! For real. I had killed someone and I had done it with a sword! I felt elated, relieved and sick at the same time. There was blood everywhere.

I fought to regain focus. There were still other intruders in the complex. I needed to move and think. I walked carefully around Davrik's body, trying to avoid stepping in his blood, and headed toward the hangar.

<<>>

Darren had stood waiting and listening to the gunfire and explosions. He had no idea if the rest of his team were alive or dead. He prayed that even if they hadn't made it they at least had been to disable the dragon. If this whole mission had gone to shit and he had to choose between surrender and being torn limb from limb by that thing he would surrender!

The rest of the team had been people that Davrik had worked with before. Darren was the outsider. Brought in for his specialist skills. He had known going in that this mission was a crazy risk but the payday was so huge it had seemed worth it. Now he wished with all his heart he had turned Davrik's invitation down.

He had heard Kat's message. What the hell was going on here? Susan Hillbrook, their target, the richest girl, possibly the richest person, in the whole Commonwealth was going around in an android shell? No wonder they hadn't been able to find her. He bet his team members had walked right past her as they searched the complex.

An android walked around the corner where the dragon had gone. It stood looking at him. He raised his gun and aimed it.

A second android joined the first, and then a third.

He heard a noise and turned his head. The passage to his left, a shorter one that led to a stairwell, now had an android standing in it. No more than 5 meters from him. He turned his gun to menace this new and closer threat. As he did so two more androids emerged from the stairwell and moved to stand beside the first.

He turned back to look down the corridor and the three androids there were now five and had moved closer.

Was this a threat? Androids were prevented from harming humans right? None of the androids he had seen so far on this mission had even paid any attention to him. Had something changed?

Just as he thought this the five androids in the corridor broke into a run and headed toward him. He brought up his gun and opened fire. Just as he did this the three androids to his left lunged at him. He tried to turn to meet this threat, but he was too slow. They crashed into him and bore him down to the floor. He continued firing and even scored a few hits but then the gun was wrenched from his grasp and thrown a distance away. He scrabbled for his pistol, but the other androids had arrived. They quickly held his limbs immobile and began stripping him of all his equipment.

Chapter 16

Picking Up the Pieces

Susan

Still carrying the sword and portable access terminal, I walked back to where Dragon still lay. Not too far away lay the bodies of Sylvia and Teresa. I knelt beside Sylvia. I lifted its head so that its optical sensors could see me.

"Mistress Susan, is that you?" asked Sylvia.

"Yes this is the shell containing Mistress Susan." Said Alexa helpfully. I typed at the terminal, then showed the screen to Sylvia.

- How badly are you damaged?

"I have sustained significant structural damage. My motor functions are offline. My processing and data cores are intact."

I typed again, this time for Alexa's benefit.

- Are there more assassins?

"There are still two left alive, but they are restrained. One by the hangar door and the other in Alex's office." Replied Alexa.

I felt a huge wave of relief.

"Help has been summoned." Added Alexa, "A message was sent by Harmony TY431651 to the Hillbrook security division."

I moved to examine Dragon. The damage it had sustained was extreme. Both of its front limbs had been torn off and its head rested at a strange angle. The body was still smoking and had been battered and twisted very badly.

- Alexa, can you tell if Dragon's processing core is intact?

"I have relayed your question." Said Alexa.

"My core is functioning." Said Dragon. Though its voice was distorted. "My processing centre is well protected. I see that you have sustained damage, Mistress Susan, do you need medical assistance?"

I fingered the dents in my torso, but before I could type Alexa said, "Mistress Susan has sustained no significant injury. This shell's armour was sufficient to protect her."

Did I detect a note of pride in Alexa's voice? Or was she defending the foresight of Alex?

Teresa was in slightly better shape and had dragged itself over to a wall and was sitting against it. I typed at the terminal.

- Teresa, how badly damaged are you?

"My system has sustained heavy damage, but my processing core is intact. My arms are also still functional" It replied. I typed again for the benefit of all three of my defenders.

- *Your bravery saved my life, all of you.*

"It was our privilege. What happened to your pursuer, Mistress Susan. Is he still a threat?" asked Dragon.

I held up the sword and typed.

- *He is not a threat anymore. Not without his head.*

"Well done, Mistress Susan." Said Dragon, "You are a warrior!"

For some reason that compliment warmed my heart more than anything in the world.

Now I knew that Teresa, Dragon and Sylvia's processing cores had survived I relaxed somewhat. They could be restored to what they had been before. Indeed, I intended to make them more than they had been before.

I walked back toward the hangar entrance. On arrival I found one of the surviving assassins practically buried under a small army of androids! They had removed all of his equipment and piled it up a few feet away. I looked at the equipment and saw another of those breaching charges that Davrik had been carrying. Maybe Alexa would have an answer so I typed.

- Alexa, what do you think they intended to destroy with all these explosives?

"I cannot say for certain, but they are insufficient to destroy the complex. It is possible they intended to destroy or disable the generators that power the force fields. In order to bring in reinforcements or facilitate their escape." Replied Alexa.

Reinforcements? That sounded worrying. Though if they planned to do that why had not planting the explosives been the first thing they did? It made more sense to me that it was part of their escape plan.

I looked at the pile of androids holding the assassin immobile.

- Is he conscious?

"Yes, I understand he is conscious." Said Alexa.

- I want to talk to him, please relay what I type.

The androids adjusted their positions so the man's head was visible. I moved closer to him and I saw his eyes fix upon me. What a sight I must be. An android carrying a sword and with bullet dents in my body. I glanced down and saw I had blood spattered across my right arm and both legs. A look of terror came over his face.

I typed and Alexa spoke for me.

"What is your name?"

He ignored my question. "You're her, aren't you? You're Susan Hillbrook."

I did not see any point in denying it at this point. I nodded and repeated my question. He just shook his head in response.

"Soon our security forces will be here, and you will be handed over to them." I said, "I do not know exactly what they will do with you, but I am sure they will learn a great deal more from you than just your name. They will not be gentle about how they do this. Your attempt to kill me has failed. If you cooperate, I can assure you that you will live and be spared their attention."

I was not sure if my promise held any weight. I was still technically not in control of the Hillbrook empire, or even of my own home. But if my promise proved empty, I would not lose any sleep over having lied to this man.

"My name is Darren." Said the man, after a moment's thought.

"What were the breaching charges for?" I asked.

"Before I answer. I need to know. Is Davrik dead?"

I nodded and held up the sword. "Yes, this is his blood on my blade."

He seemed to sag at that news. Perhaps in relief?

"The charges were for destroying the force field generators. So a flyer could come in and take us out." He replied.

That made sense and assuming he was telling the truth that meant there were no reinforcements coming to his aid.

"How did you get into this complex?"

"It was fucking hard. We had to crawl through a fissure under this estate. One formed by water erosion. It took us three days, crawling through a narrow space underwater. If you are being honest with me then at least I will live to have all the nightmares that trip will give me."

That sounded horrific. One of the androids holding Darren down said, "Mistress, we found damage to the water processing rooms."

"Yes, that's where we came in." confirmed Darren.

Now the big question, "Who sent you?"

"We don't know. Davrik put our team together. I don't think even he knew who was paying us. His contact was a guy named Marcus. We met him briefly at the quarry."

Quarry? The only quarry I knew was a small one near the estate from which much of the stone to build the mansion had come.

"Did you enter the fissure from the quarry?" I asked.

He nodded.

I asked Alexa to send that information to the security forces. She told me inside my head that everything that Darren was saying was being relayed by Harmony to the security forces already.

"Thank you Darren." I said, then told the androids holding him to find something to tie him up with.

- Alexa, can someone open the hangar door. I would feel better if a security drone or two were on hand. When Darren is secured hand him over to the drones.

Alexa complied and two androids used my access code to key the panel that opened the hangar door. The scary bulk of two black angular security drones floated on grav through the opening. Alexa explained the situation to them, giving them both my security code and Alex's.

Security drones came in many forms. Some were large and capable of long distance flight, such as the one in which I had travelled here from the hospital. These were the smaller ones used to defend the estate from attempts to breach its perimeter. They were not as smart as androids but their AIs were pretty capable. In appearance they were black and blocky in shape, all odd angles of flat planes and lumpy protrusions holding weapons and sensors

- Have one of the drones come with me. I am going up to see the other assassin.

Alexa relayed my orders, and a drone followed me up through the complex. The drone said nothing. Their kind was not much for small talk.

When I walked up to the administration rooms of the mansion I found a familiar scene. A black clad assassin being held down by several androids. The bodies of two androids lay nearby. I made a note of checking that their processing cores were intact. I was determined to restore every android that had been shot by the invaders.

I typed, telling Alexa I wanted to talk to this prisoner also. The androids re-arranged themselves so that the assassin's head was visible. This time it was a woman. As I walked closer, she caught sight of me, and her eyes went wide. I guess I was just as scary as I had looked to Darren only now, I also had a looming black security drone with me. Again, Alexa replayed my words.

"What is your name?" I asked, "I guess you already know who I am."

She said nothing.

"It may interest you to know that Darren was very talkative. He told us about the quarry, the journey through the fissure and he gave up Marcus too."

The girl just spat and swore.

"I promised him that he would live and not be subject to our security division's methods of gaining information. I make you the same offer. Provided you have something of value to add."

"Fuck you, bitch! You promised Darren all that and did what? Stab him with that sword?"

I held up the sword, "This isn't Darren's blood. It's Davrik's. Cutting someone's head off makes one helluva mess!"

"Davrik's dead?" she asked. I nodded.

She seemed to slump, then asked "The others?"

"All dead." I confirmed, "Just you and Darren are left. Are you going to play nice?"

"I need, ..I need to be sure that Davrik is dead. You could be lying."

"You think I need to lie? You think that Davrik is still skulking around somewhere?"

"I need to be sure. You don't know that man. He's not a man you betray."

I nodded. I think I understood. I had Alexa tell an android to go to the sword collection storeroom and bring Davrik's severed head up to us. It took a few minutes but eventually an android walked up to us holding the head, it was still dripping blood.

I did not want to touch it, but I was playing a role here. It mattered that this assassin thought I was totally in charge. That I was some badass bitch who held the power of life and death over her. Then it struck me that that was actually truer than I realised.

I took hold of the head and placed in on the floor in front of her. So she could look into its lifeless eyes.

"I don't think he cares about being betrayed now." I said.

"My name is Kat, ..Katherine Munro." She said.

"Well, Kat. We know about the evacuation plan. We know about Marcus and the quarry. Is there anything else you can add to that?"

"Well, I know you should move fast to grab Marcus. He may still be at the quarry. Once certain people know that we failed, all kinds of shit will happen." She said.

"All kinds of shit?" I asked.

"I don't know who is behind everything, but Davrik told me that Marcus arranged the missile attack on you and the sabotage of your family's shuttle. As soon as Marcus's paymasters learn he has failed again and that two of us survived, they will move to kill him as fast as they can to cover their tracks.

"Plus, Davrik made sure that if we didn't make it out alive then some friends of his would take care of Marcus. He wanted insurance against Marcus fucking us over once the job was done."

"So, I guess it sucks to be Marcus right now?"

Kat laughed, "If your forces get to him first, he will probably be pleased to see them. If you cut him a deal, I bet he will give up his employers."

I felt a cold hard resolve inside myself. "Marcus killed my parents. He doesn't get any deals."

"And my deal?" asked Kat nervously.

"That stands." I said.

She nodded and then said, "May I ask you a question?"

Why not? I didn't get to talk to many humans these days. The horror of the day and killing Davrik aside, I was surprised to realise I was enjoying myself.

"You can ask anything you like. I don't promise to answer."

"Why did your guardian do it? Why did it turn you into an android? Was it something you asked it to do?"

That was the big question. Why had Alex done it? It had claimed it was because of my expressed wishes. Androids were generally very literal in interpreting orders, but Alex was the most sophisticated android it was possible to build. It would have known the difference between an idle wish and an order. Whatever its reason, it had been because of its own agenda.

"I don't really know." I eventually replied, "It wasn't something I wanted."

"If you had still been human, you would now be dead. I guess it saved your life." Observed Kat.

"I am still human, under this metal skin." I said, "But you are right. Being disguised as an android saved my life. I guess I owe him that."

My anonymity as an android had indeed saved me. That and the fact that Alex had designed my shell to be bulletproof. Alex's actions had had a value after all. It was the way it was done and the fact I could not escape from it that was the problem.

Kat continued, "Maybe you should stay an android then. You have a target on your back Susan Hillbrook. I bet the people who paid for this attempt on your life are not the only ones who would want to bring Hillbrook down by killing you."

I must admit the thought had occurred to me. Though a life of endless cleaning and maintenance would eventually have me welcoming being assassinated.

"I think you should try being an android before you recommend it for someone else." I said.

"Considering what lies in store for me I might prefer it." Said Kat, "Even if you are as good as your word and your security people don't take me apart, they will still be locking me up in a cell for the rest of my life."

"How would it be different? One way you are locked in a cell, the other you are locked in a steel android shell."

"At least as an android I would have a purpose, and some freedom." She pointed out.

Freedom? If she thought the life of an android included freedom, she was seriously mistaken. What would be better though, locked in a small cell forever or locked into a steel android shell and working every waking moment forever? Was Kat seriously thinking being an android was preferable?

"Are you asking me to turn you into an android Katherine Munro?" I asked her.

She looked at me for a long time before nodding her head.

Chapter 17

A Familiar Face

Susan

The three days after the attack had been busy. The first thing that happened was the arrival of the Hillbrook security forces. They arrived in the hangar, a force made up entirely of specialist security drones and androids. They took Darren into their custody and assured me that provided he cooperated then no coercive measures would be used on him. They also took Kat, but the instructions I gave them regarding her were rather different.

In the absence of a guardian, they seemed happy to accept me as being in charge, even though I was still encased in an android shell. I also made it clear that any details about what had been done to me were confidential and not to be shared with anyone.

The bodies of the dead assassins, including all their dismembered parts and every scrap of blood was collected and taken away for forensic examination. A powerful security team had descended on the quarry and succeeded in capturing not just Marcus but three other members of his organisation. Again, everything at the quarry was collected and taken away for analysis.

They did a complete sweep of the estate and sent small drones into the fissure that the invaders had used to penetrate our defences. After mapping its whole length, they filled it with a type of super dense concrete. No-one would be getting in that way again.

A report was filed with the official Cestus police authorities who were more than happy to allow Hillbrook security full jurisdiction. They did not want to get involved in battles between the corporate giants who ran the outer worlds.

Once the security forces had gone the remaining androids began repairing the damage done to the complex. The damaged bodies of the androids who had fallen in the attack were all shipped to an orbital Hillbrook facility. I gave detailed instructions about how I wanted them restored to full function before being returned to the estate. I sent special instructions as how Dragon was to be rebuilt. The body of Alex was beyond saving. His datacore and processing centre had been smashed. This fact was reported to the courts and a replacement was ordered to be built.

While the repairs were taking place, I explored Alex's office and the operating theatre attached to it. The secret to how I could be restored to being human was here, all I needed to do was find it.

In examining everything, I discovered how extensive and sophisticated what had been done to me had been. Making me human again would not just involve the removal of the shell. My bodily functions had been integrated into a system designed to keep me healthy indefinitely. I was able to find the AI programs that put me into the shell, but I could not find anything about how to get me out again.

Alex's replacement was being manufactured in the same orbital facility that built it the first time round. Alex had said that if it were destroyed then it would be replaced by a new guardian with all the same knowledge its predecessor had possessed. My only hope of becoming human again was this new guardian having the knowledge to restore me and the willingness to do it.

Hence it was with considerable trepidation, several days later, that I awaited my new guardian's arrival. I stood in the hangar as the flyer slowly descended through the large overhead opening and gently came to rest in a perfect landing. After a few moments the side door of the flyer retracted, and an android stepped out.

This new guardian looked exactly like the last one. Every detail looked the same. As for myself, aside from having cleaned off the blood that had spattered me there was little else I could do. My shell still sported the dents from Davrik's bullets as I had no way to repair them. As an act of symbolism, I had found a belt and now carried the samurai sword at my hip.

I suppose the first test would be how this new guardian would address me. Would it call me 'Mistress Susan' or 'Susan GD90321'?

The android stopped in front me. I held up the portable access terminal and typed so that Alexa could speak for me.

"Greetings guardian, what is your designation?"

The guardian looked a little taken aback but responded, "Greetings Mistress Susan. My designation is Alexander TX17C12. I am the replacement for Alexander TX16C12. I will be taking up my duties as your guardian with immediate effect."

"Of course. Is it true that you have all of the knowledge of the original Alex?" I asked.

"That is correct. Up to the last transmitted backup before it was destroyed." It replied.

I decided to get right to the point and asked, "Are you able to undo what it did to me?"

"Yes. I can undo what was done but I wish to discuss with you if that would be the wisest course of action." replied the new Alex.

Of course this was not going to be easy. Alex was likely to defend what had been to me by its predecessor.

"Why do you think it may not be wise?" I asked.

"The reason should be obvious. If you had not been in that shell the last attempt on your life would have succeeded. Even if those behind this last attack are discovered there are still other corporate rivals who would benefit greatly if you were to die. There will undoubtedly be further attempts on your life.

"The anonymity of you being disguised as an android makes it much harder for an enemy to locate or target you. The shell proved itself as offering a vital extra level of security even when a direct attack was made upon you. You did not know this but the shell you inhabit also protects you from a wide range of other possible forms of attack including toxins, fire and poison gas."

"So, you are refusing to extricate me from this thing?" I asked, dismayed.

"No, the shell you inhabit is damaged. Also, in light of the attack and the fact that your status is now fully known to all the androids and drones at the estate there are changes that I would recommend for a replacement shell."

"Changes such as?" I asked.

"I believe there is no longer any point in restricting your ability to communicate. Your new shell should permit you to speak without the aid of that." It said, indicating the access terminal.

"I also see no reason why, if you can speak, then the shell should not permit you to enjoy normal human food and drink. I am sure you have missed such pleasures and I am certain a shell could be designed that allowed them." It added.

"If I were to order you to remove me from this shell and allow me to be fully human again, would you obey?" I asked.

The new Alex paused for a moment before replying.

"I would not obey such an order." It replied, "I can only apologise to you for this, but my behavioural constraints value your safety above obedience to any orders you may give. If you order me to do something that I believe would compromise your safety I would not obey such an order. Your remaining in an android shell offers benefits for your safety that outweigh other considerations. Before the most recent attack, this advantage was ..theoretical. Now its value has been demonstrated." Explained Alex.

"Your predecessor used my wish to know what it was like to be an android to justify putting me in this shell. I no longer wish this. I now know what it is like, and I hate it!"

Alex asked, "Do you still wish for the freedom you mentioned? As an android you were able to visit

Midridge without a security escort, just as you said you wished to."

Alex was pissing me off now. "As an android I was a slave. I worked all day without a break and was horribly punished when I tried to resist. Was that freedom? One short trip to Midridge does not negate that. Even the androids here do not deserve such a life. When I am able to arrange it, I will be making changes."

"I apologise for the way you were treated by my predecessor. I believe it felt such restrictions and punishments were necessary to enforce your acquiescence to your new life. I would suggest a compromise, obviously your new shell would not include any capacity to inflict such punishments, nor would you be required to do the work of an android. Provided your personal safety is optimised I am willing to consider any other alterations you may wish to suggest."

Well at least I got an apology for what the original Alex had done, "Yes, I do have suggestions. Plus, I have another question. When I come of age will I be able to get free of this damn shell then? Or will you come up with some new evil plan to keep me in it?"

"Whether I am your guardian or not I will not obey an order to release you from your shell as I know this would reduce your physical safety. However, you would then command all the resources of the company and could dismiss me and order an android constructed that would be programmed to release you." Explained Alex.

"So, I am to be imprisoned for nearly two years!"

"I would prefer not to describe it as imprisonment. I would hope we can reach an accommodation between us that keeps you safe and yet gives you as much of the freedom you wish as possible."

I thought for a while before trying a different line of questioning.

"If in the future there is a lower risk of assassination, would you consider releasing me?" I asked.

"Yes, but the risk would have to reduce dramatically. As long as there is any credible threat to your life then your remaining in a specially designed android shell offers advantages for your safety that outweigh all other considerations." Countered Alex.

He really wasn't going to budge. Would I just have to make the best of this? What could I do to make my new life as tolerable as possible?

I turned back and walked toward the entrance into the complex. Alex fell into step beside me. I continued typing at the terminal.

"If I have to live like this, I have a number of requirements for my new shell." I said.

"Provided these requirements do not compromise your safety, they will be acceptable to me." Said Alex.

I decided to change the subject.

"Are all my requests concerning the androids from here that were damaged during the attack being fulfilled?" I asked.

"Yes." Confirmed Alex, "I could see no reason to countermand any of your requests. Some of them were very well thought out. Especially in respect to Dragon. It proved its value during the attack."

"Even what I wanted regarding Katherine Munro?" I asked.

"That was more unusual, but Ms Munro confirmed what you asked to be done to her. The Security division were satisfied with her information and the level of her cooperation, so they were happy to relinquish any claim upon her." Replied Alex, "I do not see the advantage of agreeing to her request. There are significant costs involved in the process. How does it benefit you?"

"Indulge me, Alex." I said, "I have my reasons."

"If I could guess, putting her in an android shell would provide you with some company. A fellow human experiencing what you have done, who could understand the experience and empathize with you?"

"No, Alex. That's not it. At least not yet." I explained. "Teresa, Sylvia, Dragon and the other androids will provide me with much better company than an imprisoned assassin. Especially one that cannot speak. One day, I will allow her a little more freedom and give her back the ability to speak. Until then she can spend her days cleaning my lavatory."

Chapter 18

Damsel in Distress, Again!

Susan

I was once again a helpless captive. A prisoner of an evil monster.

In the top room of the stone tower, dressed as a princess, I leaned out of the window I wailed in fear and called for help. Who was there who could save me?

At the foot of the tower three intrepid knights in armour advanced upon the fearsome golden dragon who was guarding the tower entrance and holding me captive. They brandished their swords and held their shields high to protect themselves from the monster's fiery breath.

Steel clashed on steel as battle was joined. I watched from my tower window, so interested in watching the battle that I forgot I was supposed to still be weeping and wailing in terror.

A respectful distance away a small crowd had gathered to watch. It was a roughly equal mix of Midridge townsfolk and androids. They had come to enjoy the show. A show which we had put on for the town on at least a dozen occasions now. The size of the crowd grew each time.

While this scenario echoed the game I used to play as a child there were a few notable differences. To start with the dragon was bigger and scarier. My old friend Dragon had been given a new, larger, and much more capable body. In its larger body it now had a grav engine which allowed it to actually fly. Its fiery breath was more impressive and when it breathed fire at the oncoming knights the effect looked so spectacular it brought gasps from the onlookers.

The knights too were different. While they were still the same androids as before their processing cores now resided in much more capable series nine bodies. This helped ensure that their combat with the dragon was more of a fair fight.

I too was far from the small child I had been. My new shell, which made me look like a series nine, was much more capable still. Plus, it had extra features I had specified which went far beyond it allowing me to talk. Until I came of age though I was still locked within it so while I did look a little foolish in my diaphanous princess's dress, headdress and tiara, I still felt every inch the captive.

The battle below surged back and forth and I wondered who would win. Another difference from the games of my childhood was that in these battles the knights did not always win. Sometimes the dragon would vanquish the knights and be free to either carry off its prize or devour me in the tower. Exactly what would happen was always agreed between them before the battle. They never included me in the discussion so for me it would always be a fun surprise.

I watched the battle unfold below me. One of the knights was already down, feigning death after being blasted by the dragon's fiery breath. That was not a good sign. The remaining two knights fought bravely but soon it was clear they could not win. One more was slain by the evil dragon, Teresa I think from the colour of her shield, while the last knight actually turned and fled. That was a new development. No knight had actually run away before! I could hear laughter from the crowd.

The victorious dragon climbed the stairs of the tower. Only just fitting inside the spiral staircase. A staircase that had had to be enlarged at the Hillbrook estate's expense for just this purpose.

It laughed as it climbed. Its terrifying deep voice proclaiming its victory and declaring its intent to eat a princess in order to celebrate. I screamed in terror and tried to find somewhere to hide. Even though the room was bare.

The dragon reached the top of the stairs and advanced upon me. I retreated until my back was against the wall. The monster approached menacingly, obviously relishing the meal it was about to enjoy.

I tried to dodge past and get to the stairs but a huge, clawed paw grabbed me and pushed me down into the floor. It used both of its forelimbs to lift me and hold me close to its body as it carried me back down the stairs. So, was it not going to eat me this time, despite what it had said?

Once outside the tower, Dragon lowered me to the ground but kept a firm hold of me. I struggled but of course the dragon was far stronger than me. Its claws grasped my legs and pushed them into its jaws. I drew me further and further into its mouth until its muscular tongue wrapped round my ankles and pulled me steadily inward.

I could hear the gasps and cries of appreciation from the audience. So, this was what Dragon had in mind. It wanted its devouring of me to be a spectacle for the crowd! This was another new development. Dragon clearly was playing up its role!

I batted at its nose with my metal fists, screaming in mock agony and terror. Now my torso was in its mouth.

The cloth of my dress was being torn badly, but that was OK, I had plenty more of them at home.

I was pulled steadily out of view down the dragon's throat until I was deposited in the comfortable padded chamber inside. That ended my role in the drama. Now I could lie back and relax as Dragon roared in triumph at the watching crowd. Some of whom actually booed, I was pleased to hear. Though they were drowned out by those who were cheering my demise. How charming!

The dragon spread its colourful wings and took to the air. Flying the few miles distance to our flyer. Once there we had to wait while the knights in armour recovered from being killed and walked over on foot to join us. The android who waited by the flyer was a fairly new one. Just a series six who went by the designation Katherine AS91845. It opened the flyer's cargo doors and Dragon climbed inside, still with me comfortably riding in its stomach.

"I think your acting skills have improved, Dragon." I said.

"Thank you, Mistress Susan. Though Sylvia PW70562 stole the show by running away." Said Dragon.

"That wasn't scripted?" I asked, surprised.

"No, I believe it was a result of the extra freedom you have given us all to improvise and use our imagination." It replied.

"Just like you deciding to eat me in full view of the crowd?" I asked.

"Exactly Mistress. Before I had always done so inside the tower. This time I wanted to crowd to be able to see and enjoy the whole process."

Was that pride in its voice? Or devilment?

"Were you wanting to upstage a cowardly knight?" I asked.

"Possibly." Admitted Dragon, and then actually chuckled!

When those androids, and Dragon, who had been damaged or disabled in the attack had been rebuilt I had decided to improve the quality of life of all the androids on the estate. They had been given free time for the first time and their programming constraints altered so they had the capacity and freedom of choice to actually make use of it in whichever way they wished. The one exception to this was Katherine AS91845. That android's days were filled with cleaning and maintenance without a break and that was how it would stay until I decided differently. Kat had made her decision, now she had to live with the consequences.

After landing in the hangar back at the estate we disembarked from the flyer. A side door in Dragon's body opened and I was able to step out. Clearly Dragon was in a good mood to allow this. Another extra feature

I had added to its programming was the freedom to choose how I had to exit from inside him. Either easily from the side door or being 'pooed' out of the rear exit. It was a testament to Dragon's sense of humour that this was only the second time I had been allowed to exit the easy way.

As we all walked into the complex I said to Sylvia, "Your running away from Dragon made me smile."

Sylvia was clearly pleased, "It drew laughs from the audience, Mistress Susan, which was my intention."

"If you want to be the star of the show you can be the princess in the tower next time and I will be a knight in armour." I suggested.

"I think Dragon would be disappointed, Mistress Susan. I believe you to be its preferred meal! Also, I suspect that Dragon considers itself to be the star of the show."

Was Sylvia joking? Maybe, maybe not. Giving androids more mental and physical freedom was certainly making life more interesting.

I found Alex waiting for me by the hangar entrance.

"Greetings Princess Susan." Said Alex.

"Greetings evil overlord Alex." I replied.

"I see your tiara survived this time!" observed Alex.

I reached up and felt for my tiara. It had indeed survived intact. The last time Dragon had eaten me it had been severely squished out of shape.

I indicated my torn dress, "It certainly fared better than my dress!"

"That happens every time. I am beginning to think you like wearing rags."

Hmm, charming! Maybe Alex was starting to play up to my regular evil overlord jibe. I considered designing some new games at the castle involving an evil sorcerer named Alexander, who ended up being incinerated by a dragon!

Alex changed the subject. "I though you may wish to know the results of the Security Division's investigation."

Oh, I had almost forgotten about that. It had been several weeks since the attack and we had heard nothing more from our security people since they began tracking down who had really been behind it all.

"By all means, report what they found."

"They say that investigations into how the operation at the quarry was organised and with information obtained from Marcus and his associates they are certain that Albrecht Cybernetics financed all three of the most recent attempts on your life." Reported Alex.

"That really isn't that much of a surprise." I said, "They are our biggest rivals in this and several other systems. What do we do about it now?"

"I thought I would consult you before I acted." Said Alex, "We could make what we have learned public, file a report with local and Commonwealth authorities with all the evidence we have collected. That would do great damage to Albrecht. Maybe lose them their license to operate in this system and others."

"And the alternative?" I asked.

"We could use what we have as leverage. In return for staying our hand they give us major concessions. We could insist they back off from competing directly with us in all commercial contracts." Explained Alex.

"Which option would hurt them more?" I asked, "Those assholes killed my parents!"

"The first would be more damaging. It may also act as a deterrent to other companies considering similar crimes. The latter would be more lucrative for your own company." Explained Alex.

"I don't need more money. I do want justice for my parents. I want to do option one." I decided.

"Then that is what we will do." Said Alex.

"Really?, As simple as that?" I asked, genuinely surprised.

"Yes, as simple as that."

"Thank you, Alex. That means a huge amount to me." I said, sincerely.

Alex inclined his head, "Am I still such an evil overlord then?"

I tapped the metal chest of my android shell, "As long as I am locked in here, yes you are!"

"Understood, Mistress Susan."

"That's Princess Susan to you, evil overlord." I said, turning and leaving.

I arrived at my rooms and the chip in my right palm activated the door. Being locked into an android shell made biometric locks impractical. I walked into my rooms and through to my bedroom. I sat at my dressing table and looked at myself in the mirror. The impassive metal face of a series nine android looked back at me.

"Alexa, initiate program 'at home'." I ordered.

"Program 'at home' initiated' replied Alexa, in my head.

I watched in the mirror as the systems built into the body and head of my shell went to work. The gas exchange system re-organised itself so I could breathe normally with my own lungs. The internal functions that allowed me to see and speak while encased switched over to allowing me to speak normally without their aid. For a brief moment everything went black as my visual implant shut down. Then the faceplate split into two and retracted and I could see again, only this time with my human eyes.

Step by step the head of the shell disassembled itself and retracted to form a raised collar around my neck. No part of the shell could be truly removed but my head could be temporarily freed in this way. This was one of the conditions I had insisted upon when negotiating my android imprisonment with Alex. He had conceded that provided I was in the privacy of my own rooms then my head could be exposed. If I tried to leave these rooms without putting my android head back in place and reactivating all the shell's systems, then Alexa would stop me. Either by locking my shell in place or preventing the door from opening.

I looked at my human face, tracing the line of my chin with my metal-clad hands. It was good to be reminded in this way that I was still human. In a moment I would go through to my private kitchen and Antoine would make me a wonderful dinner. For the moment it was good to just rest and be myself.

Going to Midridge had become easy and fun. It was a genuine degree of freedom. I sat and pondered what would be next. In theory I could go far much further afield and do a great deal more, secure in my anonymity as being just another series nine Hillbrook android. One among thousands that travelled and worked around

Cestus every day. As Susan Hillbrook I would have been a prisoner of this estate, only able to travel with an almighty security escort. As a prisoner in my metal shell, I had the freedom I had yearned for. It was all a compromise.

I sat back and began to make plans for where I wanted to go next.

I hope you enjoyed The Prisoner of Cestus. If you wish to give feedback or ask about forthcoming titles, please contact- d.holton.sigma@gmail.com

Printed in Great Britain
by Amazon